The Book of Disappearance

Middle East Literature in Translation
Michael Beard and Adnan Haydar, *Series Editors*

Select Titles in Middle East Literature in Translation

The Candidate: A Novel
    Zareh Vorpouni; Jennifer Manoukian
    and Ishkhan Jinbashian, trans.

A Cloudy Day on the Western Shore
    Mohamed Mansi Qandil; Barbara Romaine, trans.

The Elusive Fox
    Muhammad Zafzaf; Mbarek Sryfi and Roger Allen, trans.

Felâtun Bey and Râkim Efendi: An Ottoman Novel
    Ahmet Midhat Efendi; Melih Levi
    and Monica M. Ringer, trans.

Gilgamesh's Snake and Other Poems
    Ghareeb Iskander; John Glenday
    and Ghareeb Iskander, trans.

Jerusalem Stands Alone
    Mahmoud Shukair; Nicole Fares, trans.

The Perception of Meaning
    Hisham Bustani; Thoraya El-Rayyes, trans.

32
    Sahar Mandour; Nicole Fares, trans.

For a full list of titles in this series,
visit https://press.syr.edu/supressbook-series
/middle-east-literature-in-translation/.

The
Book of
Disappearance

A Novel

Ibtisam Azem

Translated from the Arabic by
Sinan Antoon

Syracuse University Press

First Edition 2019

19 20 21 22 23 24   6 5 4 3 2 1

Originally published in Arabic as *Sifr al-Ikhtifa'* (Beirut: Dar al-Jamal, 2014).

∞ The paper used in this publication meets the minimum requirements of the American National Standard for Information Sciences—Permanence of Paper for Printed Library Materials, ANSI Z39.48-1992.

For a listing of books published and distributed by Syracuse University Press, visit https://press.syr.edu.

ISBN: 978-0-8156-1111-0 (paperback)
        978-0-8156-5483-4 (e-book)

Library of Congress Cataloging-in-Publication Data

Names: 'Āzim, Ibtisām, 1974– author. | Antoon, Sinan, 1967– translator.

Title: The book of disappearance : a novel / Ibtisam Azem ; translated from the Arabic by Sinan Antoon.

Other titles: Sifr al-ikhtifa'. English

Description: First edition. | Syracuse, New York : Syracuse University Press, 2019. |

Identifiers: LCCN 2019016085 (print) | LCCN 2019017760 (ebook) | ISBN 9780815654834 (E-book) | ISBN 9780815611110 (pbk.)

Classification: LCC PJ7914.Z35 (ebook) | LCC PJ7914.Z35 S54 2019 (print) | DDC 892.7/37—dc23

LC record available at https://lccn.loc.gov/2019016085

Manufactured in the United States of America

For *Tata Rasmiyye.*
For *Sidu Mhammad, Ikhlas, Abla, and Salim.*
For *Jaffans.*

The Book of Disappearance

1

Alaa

My mother put on mismatched shoes and ran out of the house. Her curly hair was tied back with a black band. The edge of her white shirt hung over her gray skirt. Fear inhabited her face, making her blue eyes seem bigger. She looked like a mad woman as she roamed the streets of Ajami, searching for my grandmother. Rushing, as if trying to catch up with herself. I followed her out. When she heard my footsteps, she looked back and gestured with her broomstick-thin arm: go back!

"Stay home, maybe she'll come back."

"But Baba is there."

"Then go to her house, and then to al-Sa'a Square. Look for her there."

She went frantically from house to house. So tense, she looked like a lost ant. Knocking on doors so hard I was afraid she'd break her hand. As if her fist was not flesh and bones, but more like a hammer. She didn't greet whoever came out and just asked right away if they'd seen my grandmother. If no one answered, she'd take a deep breath and weep before

1

the closed door. Then she'd go on to the next house, wiping her tears away with her sleeves.

I followed her, like a child. I'd forgotten how fast her pace was. I was forty and had retained only faint and distant memories from that childhood. I was afraid she'd get hurt. I'd never seen her so overtaken by fear. She looked back every now and then, perplexed that I insisted on following her. I stayed a few steps behind. I felt too weak to challenge this woman: my mother. I begged her to go home and told her I'd search Ajami, house by house, to find Tata. She gestured again with her arm, as if I were a mere fly blocking her way. She kept searching and the houses spat her out, one by one.

I had gone home to our house in Ajami about an hour earlier to catch the sunset in Jaffa. I go twice a week, usually two hours before sunset, and wait until we are all sleepy before heading back to my apartment in Tel Aviv. Tata had moved to live with my parents six months earlier. Mother insisted that she move in after having found her unconscious in her bathroom, her leg almost broken.

Tata's house on al-Count Street was just a ten-minute walk away. "Al-Count" is the old name Tata still insisted on using. I had put "Sha'are Namanor" on the mailbox. What am I saying? She didn't "insist" on using that name. That *was* its name. Al-Count sounded strange to me when I was a child. But later Tata told me that it was the honorific given by the Vatican to Talmas, the Palestinian man who donated money to build the Maronite church in Jaffa. He had lived on this street and it took his name.

After she moved to live with my parents, Tata insisted on going back every morning to water her roses and tend to them. Mother would accompany her and she or my father would later go back, just before sunset, to bring Tata back home. That morning Tata said she felt a bit tired and didn't go to her house. She went out alone, which was unusual, an hour after mother did. That's what my father said when I got home. When my mother came back after visiting a friend and buying a few things she was terrified.

The day squandered its minutes before my eyes. I was tired of following my mother, so I left her and hurried to al-Sa'a Square. Tata loved it. We called her Tata, not *sitti*. She didn't like *sitti*.

But then I came back. She won't be there. There was no place to sit and look at Jaffa there. I figured that she must've gone to the shore, the one near the old city. She loved that spot. So I hurried toward the sea, to the hill where she liked to sit. To get there quickly, I had to go through the artists' alleyways in the old city. I hated walking through them.

Will I find her? Will I find Tata? I felt my heart choking.

I heard my breath stumbling as I went through the narrow alleyways between the dollhouses. That's what I used to call the artists' galleries there. I felt a sudden pain in my chest as I ran up the old steps. As if my lungs had become narrow, just like those alleyways. When I used to pass through old streets as a child I would see my shadow walking next to other shadows. Sometimes it would leave me, as if it had become someone else's shadow. I thought I was crazy and kept this a secret for years. Once I was with Tata and I asked her to take another route that doesn't go through the old city. She laughed, kissed my head, and held my hand. "Don't be scared, *habibi*. All the Jaffans who stayed here see a shadow walking next to them when they walk through the old city. Even the Jews say they hear voices at night, but when they go out to see who it is, they don't find anyone."

Her story didn't help me knock out my fear. It overwhelmed me and still haunted me even as I got older. I reached the open square overlooking the sea. The sea surprises me every time I come here after escaping the jaws of the old city's alleyways. I felt a dry wind touching my lips as though in a desert. The sea is before me, yet I feel I am in a desert. I looked north, beyond Jaffa. The glass windows of the other city, the white city, the city of glass, shot their reflections back at me.

I headed to the hill next to Mar Butrus Church. I felt the church, too, was tired.

I found her.

She was sitting on the wooden bench, looking at the sea. I called out loud, happiness lilting in my voice as I ran toward her: "Tata! Tata! Tata!" I looked at her tan face gazing at the sea. A strand of black hair had managed to slip away from her headscarf, as if to dance with the wind. A light smile perched on her lips. I sat next to her and held her hand. "You scared us to death!" Her fingers were wooden, dry even though her body did not feel cold, to me at least. When I shook her shoulder, she leaned a bit. I held on to her shoulder again with my shaking fingers. Had she fainted? I placed my ear on her chest to see if she was breathing. I felt suffocated, as if all of Jaffa was caged in my chest. I took out my cell phone to call for an ambulance. I could barely force words out of my dry mouth. All that water around me, yet my mouth was still so dry.

She was sitting on the old wooden bench gazing at the sea. Surrounded by the noise of the children playing nearby. "Children are the birds of paradise," she used to say. Mother would shoot back, "God save us from such birds. They're all noise and no fun. Oh God, will there be noise in paradise too?" None of the passersby noticed that she had died. She died just the way she'd wanted: either in her bed, or by the sea. She used to pray that she'd never get so old to need anyone's help. "Please, God, don't let me be dependent on anyone. Take me to you while I am still strong and healthy." I inched closer and hugged her. Perhaps she was the one hugging me at that moment. I knew it would be our last moment alone, before the ambulance came. I could smell jasmine, her favorite scent. She surrounded herself with tiny bottles of it, everywhere in her house. I didn't shed any tears. Perhaps I had yet to comprehend what had happened.

Or maybe I didn't want to believe that she had died. The only meaning that word had at that moment was a strange and overwhelming sense of emptiness. I called my father. He said mother was back at home and on the verge of madness. They were going to follow me to the hospital.

She took a bath before going out. As if going to her own funeral.

2

Alaa

"I lived my life, lonely," she used to say. Even though her house was always full of guests, as I remember. But memory is dense fog that spreads or clears as one gets older. I never understood why she spoke of herself in the past tense so often. Even when she laughed, and she loved to laugh, she would still speak of herself in the past tense and would say, "I used to love laughing. Oh, how I loved laughing!"

Tata died.

I still get goose bumps whenever I say it. Tata died. I was relieved that she died without needing anyone. But she died.

She died.

She took a bath before leaving the house.

As if going to her own funeral!

She was sitting in the middle of the wooden bench, facing the sea. She was wearing her purple plissé skirt, and a matching shirt under her black chiffon coat. Without her tiny black purse this time. Or maybe someone stole it from her? How did she get here? A see-through black scarf hid her hair. She never let it go white and would always dye it black. Even after reaching her seventies, she would still paint her nails, making sure the colors matched her attire. "No one loves life the way we, the people al-Manshiyye, and of the sea, do." She would always mock those who didn't groom themselves, as if only city folk and Jaffans knew how to do so.

She liked to sit by the sea, often on the Arab beach, near Ajami. But she loved that other spot atop the hill where I found her, too, especially the wooden bench. I never knew why. And she died here, by the sea. She preferred to die in Jaffa rather than leave. Whenever she mentioned Jaffa's name, she would take a deep breath, as if the city had, all of a sudden, betrayed her and scorched her heart. At that moment, when I saw that her body was a corpse gazing at the sea, I realized that there were so many questions I had yet to ask her. But death and time beat me to them. "How many times can one say the same thing? I swear sometimes I get sick of myself," she used to say with a smile, when I asked her to retell one of her stories.

Longing for her is like holding a rose of thorns!

I noticed that she was clutching something in her right fist. When I tried to loosen her hand, I saw her pearl necklace. It had come loose in the past, but she didn't want to have it restrung. Sometimes she used to take it out of its old wooden box, where it was wrapped in cotton, just to look at it. I asked my mother about it, but she didn't know anything, or if the pearls were real or fake. I had a feeling she wasn't telling the truth.

Tata had a black beauty mark on her right cheek, like the bezel of a precious ring. When I was a child I used to reach up to touch and kiss it. Mother has one, too, on her left cheek. When I looked at Tata's face there was a light smile still alive, showing some of her teeth. "I don't wear dentures," she used to say, "No one believes that I am over eighty and don't need them. My feet ache because of the sewing machine, but my teeth are like pearls."

Why did Tata choose to die alone, facing the sea? Was she always lonely, even when she was with us? Something about survivors leaves them always lonely.

"I walk in the city, but it doesn't recognize me," she once said in a sad voice.

"Why would the city recognize you, Tata? It's not like you're Alexander the Great. You know the city is inanimate! It's not a person."

"What are you saying? Who told you a city cannot recognize its people? You kids don't understand anything. A city dies if it doesn't recognize its people. The sea is the only thing that hasn't changed. But frankly, it's meaningless. Lots of water for nothing."

I laughed when she said that. She would take back her insult to the sea, as if it were the only thing that remained loyal. It neither changed, nor left. She would always complain that the streets were empty. They had many people, but were still empty. "All those people left their own countries and came here. What for? They crowd everything, but have no gravitas. I don't like to walk down the street in the morning and not come across someone I know. There are only a handful of us left who can greet each other. Come, let's stop by the pharmacy to say hello to Abu Yusif."

I used to accompany her to al-Kamal Pharmacy. As soon as we enter, she would start complaining to Abu Yusif about the pain in her knees. I would remind her that he's not a physician, but he would tell me to let her ask her question. Whenever she met one of those who stayed in Jaffa, she used to regress to a little girl. They would speak of "that year" and what happened before and after "that year." When I was a teenager I used to mock the pharmacy's name and its greenish wood. But now I've learned to love it. I get all my prescriptions there. I see Tata standing or sitting there, taking her time, and talking to the pharmacist. Always about Jaffans, their names, and news. I used to get tired of all those names when I was young.

"He told me that we must leave. I've arranged everything and we must go to Beirut before they kill us all. We'll come back when things calm down. I told him that am not leaving. I'm six months pregnant. What would we do if something happened on the way there? How could one leave Jaffa anyway? What would I do in Beirut? There is nothing there. I don't like Beirut. You live in Jaffa, and think of going to Beirut? I never liked Beirut. I don't know why people like it so much. Nothing worth seeing."

Whenever *sidu*'s name came up, she used to repeat her answer to him, but would revise details here and there. Sometimes Beirut becomes beautiful, but it wasn't her city and she didn't want to go there. At other times Beirut was just a trivial hell.

"Weren't you afraid?"

"Who said I wasn't? A week before your *sidu* and my folks left, I thought I was going to have a miscarriage. The bullets were everywhere. They used to shoot at us whenever we went outside our houses. We were like mice. Our lives had no value. Why do you think everyone left the city? Do you know why my brother Rubin, my sister Sumayya, and all my uncles left? No one leaves just like that. That's enough, grandson. Don't hurt me even more."

I waited two days and then asked her again about the house. She said it's in al-Manshiyye. The building where her family lived was bombed and collapsed on top of those living in it. She was lucky that she felt severe pain that night, and her family was visiting her, so they slept over. When they went back the next morning, they didn't find their neighbors. They all perished in the rubble of the building. The building died, and they died with it. It was a coincidence that her family survived. My grandfather and her family decided to go to Beirut until things calm down. But she refused to go with them. He was convinced that she would join him later. Her mother and siblings went with him. Her father, my great grandfather, stayed with her after she refused to go. He had hoped that he would join the others, or that they would eventually return. But they weren't able to do so, and she didn't want to leave. She inherited stubbornness from her father. My grandfather waited ten years for her, but she never joined him. She would always say, "I never left. He's the one who left. I stayed in my home."

So, my mother lived without her father and never knew him. My grandfather married another woman after divorcing my grandmother. After tens of letters he had written and sent via the International Red Cross, he penned one final letter. He said in it that he would wait until the end of that year. If she didn't come, he would divorce her and set her free. And so it was, on paper at least. I asked her once if the pearl necklace was a gift from him. She laughed and didn't answer. When I asked her when did it come loose, she answered, but without answering. "People went away, a country stayed, our souls came loose, and you keep asking about the pearl necklace? I'm done this evening. Enough questions."

I wish I'd asked her more questions.

I wish I'd talked to her much more.

𝐤

Alaa put his pen down on the wooden table, whose short legs were anchored in the sandy beach. He felt some back pain, so he reclined in the orange chair. He gazed at the sea's blueness. He turned left and saw the lights of Mar Butrus Church and the Bahr Mosque.

He went back to read what he'd just written. She used to mock his chaotic script whenever she saw him writing. "Why are your scribbles like chicken marks, sweetheart? You should have seen my father's script. It was so beautiful, like a calligrapher's."

It was the first time Alaa had started writing his memoirs in the red notebook. Its color caught his eye when he was passing by a stationery store on Allenby Street. He bought it and was walking to Tsfoni Café on the beach when he decided to start writing his memoirs.

He felt exhausted and shut his big blue eyes to listen to the waves of the sea, and nothing else. But the loud reggae music billowing from the big speakers and the chatter of other customers were jamming to silence the sea. He tried, in vain, to listen to the waves.

3

Alaa

I return to you, now, two weeks after first writing in this notebook. I don't know why I begin by addressing you directly. As if you are still here, or you will actually read these words. I'm not even sure if there is life after death. Nor do I know where souls go after they depart our bodies. You might be angry with me for saying that! But I think you will laugh. Yes, that's more like you. You would ask God to forgive me. But then you would laugh and say, "All will be well." That expression used to anger me quite a bit, especially when you said it. How could someone who went through what you did, still say "All will be well." "If all wasn't well to start with, how would it be well afterward?" I used to ask you. But you would laugh and say, "Don't give me a headache. Find something else to argue about. Is this what they teach you at university? Just finish already and find yourself a wife."

I am sitting at Tsfoni Café. I always come back to this spot. Why do I like to come here? Maybe because it's right on the beach. I take off my shoes and put my feet down in the sand. There is nothing but the sea.

14

Here, Jaffa is on my left, and the sea is spread out before me. I leave Tel Aviv behind. I don't see it, and it doesn't see me. I leave its buildings and noise. The sound of the sea overpowers the sounds of the city. I know Tel Aviv is behind me, but I couldn't care less about its existence.

We didn't spend much time together, but I feel your presence everywhere in this country. What is "much" anyway? I had wanted to bring you here to this spot. Hoping you would try to remember if you, too, loved it in the past, before my grandfather left. Perhaps you two walked together here once? It's not far from your house in al-Manshiyye.

I'm mad at you. Your memory, which is engraved in my mind, has all these holes in it. Am I not remembering all that you told me, or was it incomprehensible? I was very young when I started listening to your stories. Later, when I turned to them for help, I discovered these holes. I started to ask you about them. But the more I asked, the more you got mixed up, or maybe I did. How would things not get mixed up? I was certain there was another city on top of the one we live in, donning it. I was certain that your city, the one you kept talking about, which has the same name, has nothing to do with my city. It resembles it a great deal. The names, orange groves, scents, al-Hamra Cinema, Apollo, weddings, Prophet Rubin's feast, Iskandar Awad Street, al-Nuzha Street, al-Sa'a Square . . . etc. Where do all these names come from? We would be walking and you start mentioning

other names too. Names not written on signs. I had to
learn to see what you were seeing. Akh! And all those
people. I got to know all their problems, and how
they were forced to leave Jaffa. I knew all the boring
(and at times interesting) details about their lives. I
knew all the jokes they used to tell. All this without
having even met a single one of them. And I probably
never will.

Your Jaffa resembles mine. But it is not the same.
Two cities impersonating each other. You carved your
names in my city, so I feel like I am a returnee from
history. Always tired, roaming my own life like a
ghost. Yes, I am a ghost who lives in your city. You,
too, are a ghost, living in my city. And we call both
cities Jaffa.

You were the exact opposite of the others. They
couldn't talk about their catastrophes when they take
place. Even if they dare open the gate of memory, they
would do it just a bit, and years later. You were the
opposite. The last time I asked you about how they
kicked you out of al-Manshiyye, forced you to go to
Ajami, and how you lived with the Hungarian family
they brought to share your house with you, you said,
"My tongue is worn away from words. Don't ask
me anymore! They didn't stay long in the house we
were forced to go to. We were lucky. That's enough,
grandson. What good will it do to talk about it? Even
words are tired."

You used to say that you would walk in the morning, but could not recognize the city, or the streets.

As if they, too, were expelled along with those who were forced to leave. Back then, my child eyes tried to imagine the scene the way you described it. "As if the darkness had swallowed them, and the sea took them hostage." That is how you described your days, and those people who were forced to leave and go beyond the sea. But you didn't say that the population of the city went from 100,000 down to 4,000. No, you didn't say that. You did say that you couldn't recognize your city after they'd left. What bereavement! My mind cannot process these figures. Nor can I comprehend what it means for a city to lose most of its people. I, who was born and raised in Jaffa after Jaffa had left itself.

You used to eat oranges voraciously. I thought you loved them, so I was surprised when you said that you didn't. You only started eating oranges after they forced you out of al-Manshiyye to Ajami. They fenced Ajami with barbed wire and declared it a closed military zone. Why, then, did you eat oranges if you didn't like them? Were you exacting revenge against those who were on the other side of the sea, yearning for Jaffa's oranges? You always complained that the cypresses on street sides lost their meaning after *that year*. They stood there doing nothing except dusting the sky. You used to say that and laugh. As if you knew it was meaningless. But you insisted that those trees were meaninglessly big. You didn't like the taste of oranges when you were growing up, you said. You only loved their scent and blossoms. But "after they left, everything took on another meaning, or no meaning at all . . . I began to love seeing people eat oranges, but I, myself, never liked them . . . I ate them, but never liked them. Oh, enough already! I'm tired of blathering. Let's talk about something else. You ask too many questions."

You said you used to walk down the streets laughing out loud with your father. Barbed wire surrounded you for more than ten years. No one could leave Ajami except with an official permit. They even stole Jaffa's name when they placed it under Tel Aviv's administrative jurisdiction. Is this why I dislike Tel Aviv? Did I inherit this lump in my throat from you? Why do I still live in it then? "Why shouldn't you? This is Palestine. These are Jaffa's villages and it'll always be ours," you said to me. But then you fell silent, as if talking was a painful act.

You said you went out with your father in what can only be described as a fit of madness. You walked with him and greeted strangers to fool him into believing that what he himself had said was true— that everyone had returned to Jaffa. You said he was demented and saw everyone there. Ten years had passed and he couldn't get used to his new Jaffa. Can one get used to his *nakba*? They changed street names into numbers to remind you that you were in a prison called Jaffa. As if you needed anyone to remind you of that. You said that your father saw bus no. 6 coming on time and saw his partner, Zico, giving him back the keys to the mobilia warehouse they co-owned.

You always said "mobilia" instead of "furniture," because you loved the sound of that word. Had I not seen this Zico in a photograph with my grandfather, I would've thought he was a figment of your imagination. Zico. What kind of name is that anyway? Was it his nickname? I asked you. You didn't know. He was your father's partner and they owned furniture stores in Jaffa. "They looted the country and the people, so you think they wouldn't loot furniture? Of course! And how many times have I said I don't want to talk about this. My father became demented and died of his heartache after that year. Why do you keep asking? How many times do I have to give the same answers? Please, sweetheart, for God's sake."

Then you went back to your silence.

You realized that your father was demented when he knocked on your door one cold morning. He told you that Zico had visited him during the night, and said they could go back to bring the furniture from the warehouse and reopen their stores. You didn't say anything when you heard him say that. You stopped arguing with him when he yelled and said that he wanted to go back to his home. When you told him he was at home, he accused you of lying. You didn't understand at first, but then you realized that he was demented, all at once. And you realized that he was going to die, all at once as well. You took him by the hand and walked with him in his last morning. "I walked and felt I was going to the gallows. The Israelis could have killed us. We weren't allowed to just go out whenever we pleased. There was barbed wire everywhere. We were in prison and he was determined to leave Ajami. God saved us. I don't know how. I was reciting the *Kursi* chapter from the Qur'an all the way. I was terrified." You took a deep breath after that last sentence. As if all the air in the world wasn't enough to fill your lungs. Sixty years later and you would still feel a tightness of breath when you talked about the nakba, your nakba and Jaffa's. Your Palestine. You took him by the hand and greeted the strangers as if they were the city's people. You said that God must've heard your prayers because no one stopped you to ask for permits. Passersby nodded as they responded to your greetings in a language they didn't know. As if everyone had agreed to let him bid his hometown farewell. When you returned home, he said he was going to take a bath and sleep a little. But you knew that that was it. Did he take a bath because he knew he was about to die? Did you do the same? Is that why you took a bath before leaving, and refused to let anyone come with you? You hadn't left the house for six months. Did you want to die alone, by the sea?

Survivors are lonely.

Today I put on that white shirt with silver buttons you used to like. When I put gel on my spiky hair, I noticed some white hairs. I remembered how you used to sit near the flowerbeds in the small garden with our neighbor Um Yasmeen. You used to dye your hair and tell my mother she should do the same. You chastised her for neglecting her looks. She would smile and tell you that you are puerile. Then you and Um Yasmeen would both laugh. Why didn't you teach mother to love life the way you did?

My mother cried her heart out when I called to tell her that I found you, and was in the ambulance, on my way to the hospital. When she entered the hospital, people looked at her mismatched shoes and hair. Her black scarf had fallen. She was crying silently. Gasping and crying in silence. Her eyes were so red, the white had almost disappeared. I took her in my arms. Her eyes were just like her father's—blue and vast like the sea, as you used to say. My father just stood by and wept out loud, as if weeping for the first and last time in his life. I had never seen him weep before. He said he was orphaned. You were more than just a mother-in-law to him. You were the mother and father he never knew. He only remembered their phantoms and flickers of memory.

Mother saw the smile on your face. "Oh God, she's laughing. She's dead, but still laughing." You were lying down as if you were about to get up, as you did so often, to complain of a headache, and ask someone to get you a cup of coffee. You know my mother gave away your clothes and furniture after you died. Was she taking revenge against you for leaving her? Maybe she never forgave you because she lived like an orphan, even though her father was alive. But it wasn't your fault. I told her many times, "Tata is the one who should be angry with *sidu*. How can someone leave his wife and go to Beirut?" I could never finish a conversation with her about this subject. Maybe she loved him so much, because she never knew him.

"As if the sea took them hostage."

This sentence swirled in my thoughts whenever I looked at the sea at Jaffa and remembered "that year."

Longing for you is like holding a rose of thorns!

4

Ariel

His head felt like an iron ball, too heavy for his neck to lift it off the pillow. The aspirin he took twenty minutes before didn't help. The liter of water he gulped down couldn't ease the pounding headache. He heard a rattle in the next room. He listened a bit and lit the lamp next to his bed. He scanned the room before jumping out of bed to open the door. He craned his neck in the darkness of the living room. Nothing. He turned on all the lights in the apartment. Still nothing. The rattle was gone.

Back in bed, he felt his forehead to make sure he didn't have a fever, and that the heat he was feeling might be caused by the weather. He combed his smooth brown hair with his fingers and realized it was high time for a haircut. Why did Alaa act so strange and stay silent the night before? They sat for an hour and a half and then he excused himself and said he had to go back to his apartment because he had to get up early. They both live in the same building. It was a coincidence, like their first encounter.

They had met at Natalie's party. The blond German who was uneasy about being blond and German. She was haunted by her guilt and her ancestors' crime. And everything somehow revolved around her guilt. Ariel complained to Alaa once that she talked so much about the Holocaust, one would think she was the granddaughter of one of the victims, and not of a Nazi.

Being blond was a burden because many in the White City flirted with her. Here, people love life—a life where everything rushes to the future. People in this young city are always looking for sex. As if sex is the goal to which they would cling to make sure they are alive during those respites between one war and another. Natalie realized (or discovered) that later, after living here for more than three years. She realized that it didn't have to do with her being a skinny blond with perky pomegranate breasts. It was rather that the young city's streets were filled with garrulous men waiting for something. Living in a state of perpetual waiting.

She worked as a correspondent for a TV channel. That's how she met Alaa. She sought his assistance every now and then when there was a crisis and the additional media coverage required more cameramen. Alaa was a freelance cameraman. He preferred freelancing because it provided him with a decent income while allowing him to continue his graduate studies in media at Tel Aviv University. She got to know Ariel through the weekly column he wrote for an American newspaper. They corresponded and became friends. Later, after she moved to work in another war zone, both Alaa and Ariel lost contact with her.

Last night they recalled that first meeting at Natalie's.

"Ariel! Come here. I want to introduce you to Alaa, the Arab I was telling you about. It turns out that you guys are neighbors. What a coincidence!"

Natalie spoke flowing Hebrew with an Ashkenazi accent. Alaa extended his hand to shake Ariel's. In a deliberately exaggerated Mizrahi accent, he said:

"Shalom Ariel. I am the token Arab of the party you all need so you can say you have an Arab friend. I think we met before on the stairs of our building."

Natalie was red in the face. She accused him of being too sensitive and insisted that she didn't mean anything by it. Ariel laughed and shook Alaa's hand vigorously. They had met on the stairs once and exchanged polite neighborly greetings.

The White City's parties never lack sexual energy and that party was no exception. A dark girl with chestnut hair sat next to him. He still remembers her beautiful voice but not what he said to her. The hash-induced numbness was spreading all over his body. He felt light and happy as if hovering high above everyone. The boredom he'd felt earlier had now been replaced with fits of laughter shared by the girl. She inched closer with each laugh and joke, coquettishly playing with her hair, and wetting her lips every time Alaa looked into her eyes.

He kept laughing and Ariel joined in after the hash got to him too. He laughed his way to the kitchen. He came back minutes later with a bottle of water, a plastic plate full of olives, cheese, and two glasses. He poured water for both of them. They both drank and Alaa ate two olives and a piece of cheese he didn't like. He turned to Ariel:

"You know what? I'm really tired of so-called leftists, foreigners, and everything in this city. I don't even know why I came to this party in the first place. I'm leaving. I'll see you later. You should come for coffee if you like. I'm not working tomorrow. But don't come in the morning. I'm not a morning person."

"I feel tired too. I have work tomorrow morning. I'd decided not to come, but changed my mind at the last minute. I'll use your exit as an excuse to head out. Just give me five minutes."

The twenty-minute walk back lasted an hour. They took turns cracking jokes and stopped at each intersection to harass passersby and wave to cars. How long ago was that? Three years? Maybe more?

Ariel tossed in bed recalling the previous night's details. They had spent most of it at Chez George reminiscing about that first meeting. A bit after eleven, Alaa said he was very tired and couldn't drink anymore. He had to wake up early for work. They paid the bill and headed back. They walked from Chez George at 45 Rothschild to their building at 5A in less than fifteen minutes. Although they'd downed a whole bottle of Nero d'Avola, they didn't felt tipsy.

Ariel tried to fall asleep, but kept tossing and turning. He felt insomnia hovering around his bed. He carried out the usual rituals to ward it off. He drank a cup of chamomile tea. Then he ran warm water in the tub and slipped in. He tried to read Amos Oz's latest novel. His mother had praised it and gifted him a copy, but he couldn't finish a single page. He got out of the tub, dried himself, and went back to bed. But he still couldn't fall asleep. He turned on the radio. David Broza's voice came through singing "The Woman by My Side."

The song awakened a bittersweet memory. Zohar, his ex, used to dance and sing along loudly whenever it came on. They were together for a year, but she meddled so much in his life that he felt suffocated. He broke up with her and still feels guilty about it. But he didn't miss her anymore, not the way he did in the beginning. He looked at his cell phone. It was three fifteen in the morning. His vacation starts tomorrow and there's no need to get up early. He turned it off.

5

Flower Farm

Just before sunrise, as if yawning, carnations bloomed in the plastic greenhouses. At four in the morning, Shimon's tense and raspy voice would billow, urging Maryam, the oldest and most experienced of his workers, to get to work, even before the shift had begun officially. Once the sun is high up, and the flowers are in full bloom, the crop would be ruined. They had to be plucked when stems were the longest to be ready for export.

Inexpensive foreign labor from China to Romania had flooded the market in recent years. But Shimon preferred Palestinian women from the West Bank. Despite the difficulties of securing work permits for them, they were faster and more efficient. Moreover, he didn't need to worry about finding housing or health care for them, as is done with foreign laborers. A car took them from the edge of Balata refugee camp in the morning and went through the checkpoint to drop them off at the farm. He doesn't know anything about them, or their lives, except for their full names and ID numbers, which he'd recorded. He only dealt with Maryam. Even when he needed to address the other workers, she was his messenger. When he happened to be in a good mood, he joked with them, but that was quite rare. He often chastised them and ordered them to keep plucking flowers whenever he heard chatter, or noticed that their work rhythm had slowed down a bit for whatever reason.

Maryam's days started before dawn. She woke up at three in the morning to do some housework and prepared school sandwiches for her kids. Everyone would still be asleep when she left and sat silently with the others in the car. Even the soldiers at the checkpoint on the way to Shimon's farm were sleepy. But they insisted on being sticklers and made everyone wait for a long time. She usually sat next to the driver and would look at the spectacle through the windshield. Waiting for a signal from one of the soldiers to move forward. Every single day a gesture from a soldier's hand, or his finger, decided their fate as they crossed the checkpoint from Palestine to Palestine. The despair of all the workers crossing was hidden beneath the morning calm.

When Maryam got to the farm she plunged her whole body into a sea of flowers, waiting to be plucked. Her back would bend and rise, as if it were independent of her fatigued body, or the silent morning. The white cover she used to wrap around her head and face could only repel the chemicals drenching the flowers. Their odor, and that of her own sweat, which trickled down her face and body, would soon reach her nostrils.

Her coworkers often accused her of taking Shimon's side and always coming to his defense. But all she wanted was to keep feeding the bodies waiting for her back at home. The Israelis threw her husband in jail, and when he was released, she didn't recognize him. He waited for her at home and she wasn't sure he recognized her. "They threw him out on the street after keeping him in prison for six months. No one knew where he was. He came back a mad man. I don't know what they did to him." She would say that and quickly wipe her tears away. "There is no time for sadness or pain. Come on, girls, let's finish our work, for God's sake. We don't want any trouble."

They complained about the chemicals Shimon sprayed. Badriyya once protested: "This guy drenches the flowers with chemicals. I've had so many problems with my face and skin since I started working here. I guess we should just dress like the Taliban and cover our faces and leave nothing but a sieve to avoid all these chemicals."

Maryam shushed her: "For God's sake, Badriyya. You never stop complaining. God help whoever is going to marry you. I've been working for years. I cover my face with a cloth and never had problems. Let's pluck them roses. May God pluck our lives to end this one."

Shimon used to tell them to stop blabbering when he heard them arguing. But this morning he stood alone, perplexed amid a sea of silent carnations. No whispers, complaints, or the sound of scissors severing elegant stems. Where are they? Why are they late? It's not a holiday. He thought of what he was going to lose that day because of their absence. He looked at his watch again, stumbled out of the farm, and headed to the storage room. He wanted to look at the calendar on its wall to make sure today was neither a holiday nor a feast for any sect or religious group in the country. It turned out to be just another day. He headed to the main door of the storage room, opened it, and stood watching the road leading to the farm.

He reached into the pocket of his khaki pants and took out his cell phone to call the neighboring farm and ask the owner if there were any closures in the West Bank. Maybe they couldn't cross the checkpoint. His neighbor confirmed that there was no curfew or problems at the checkpoint and said that his Arab workers were no-shows too.

Shimon was so angry he almost injured his fingers dialing the driver's number. Nidal's cell phone was lying on the kitchen table at his home, right next to a full cup of tea. The sugar at the bottom had not dissolved. The phone kept shaking as it rang. It crawled to the edge of the table with each call until it fell on the floor.

6

Bus Stop

David sat down on one of the orange plastic seats at the bus stop near al-Sa'a Square in Jaffa. He was waiting for the 5:30 a.m. bus. The cold crept into his body as he looked at the street on that calm morning. He had decided to tell Yusif about his plans to open a restaurant and urge him to agree to be his partner.

They met at the al-Karmil Market three decades earlier when they both worked there. It was a dim and cold February evening. Many vendors had closed shop unusually early. None of them earned enough to pay one worker for that unseasonably rainy day. The old buildings overlooking the market appeared as if they were about to keel over at any moment. These were the buildings of the Yemenite neighborhood, the first of the White City's colonies.

Their friendship started with an animosity they both shared against Yossi, who used to exact a fee from everyone. They tried to convince the other vendors—Yemenites, Moroccans, Iraqis, and Palestinians—to rebel and refuse to pay the fee. But this didn't bear fruit. On the contrary, the other vendors couldn't understand why Yusif and David were so concerned with the fee when they themselves were merely workers who didn't own their own stalls.

They worked across from each other. Yusif sold fruit in all seasons. Winter was on its way out that day and the scent of citrus fruits wafted all around him. He loved oranges, and used to peel one every morning and keep its peel nearby, to sniff it every now and then. David, on the other hand, worked for a vegetable vendor. He mostly sold those finger-thin local cucumbers with yellowish fez-like flowers dangling from their edges. But that was long ago, because today's cucumbers have no scent.

Jaffans don't like the people of Tel Aviv. The reason is not jealousy, as some malicious folks claim, but familiarity. You can't love something fake, Yusif used to say. The city that never rests doesn't let those around it rest either. Everything was a lie, even the name itself, Tel Aviv, meaning "the Hill of Spring." The city wasn't built on a hill. It was a shore that had no hills. But who cares? Illusion suffices to live the lie that later becomes the truth. Yusif used to get very angry whenever he heard a Palestinian say that Tel Aviv was called "The Hill of Spring" before the nakba. He would scream at them, "How are you going to liberate Palestine with this ignorance? That's what *they* called it, and there is no 'Spring Hill.' That is the Arabic translation, but not the name. Tel Aviv is merely Jaffa and the surrounding villages. That's what Tel Aviv is: Jaffa and its suburbs, no more and no less. How long will we remain ignorant of our history? Don't tell me about occupation and colonialism. What the fuck does that have to do with it? What does occupation have to do with you not knowing a simple fact?"

On that rainy day, Yusif was looking at the oranges in his stand when he heard someone asking,

"Are you Yusif Haddad?"

When he looked up he saw a burly man. No sooner than he nodded, clubs rained on him. David picked up a stick and rushed to save his neighbor. He struck the burly man, but he didn't seem to feel anything. Both Yusif and David were skinny, but they picked up every box or rock nearby and threw them at the men hitting them.

In their version, they beat the assailants to a pulp. But those who knew them back then say the opposite is true. They both ended up in hospital for a week, and never set foot in the al-Karmil Market after that.

Yusif stayed in Ajami and became a bus driver. David learned enough about cooking and became a chef at a Tel Aviv restaurant in Ramat Aviv, or as the people of oranges call that area, al-Shaykh Mwannis.

Yusif always said that he loved David like he loved his brother, who left in 1948 and disappeared. When they besieged Jaffa, Tamim went to fight and never returned. His mother said he was very handsome. Some told her that he was in Lebanon, working in the refugee camps. Others assured her that they personally saw him in Gaza. There were those who said he died. No one could prove it, or tell her to her face. Once, a neighbor who meant well told her that he was probably martyred, and a martyr is like a groom. She screamed at him and almost kicked him out of the house. "It's wrong to say that, Abu Samir. Were you there with him yourself? Do you know someone who was for you to say this? It's unacceptable."

No one ever dared broach the subject in her presence. They let her talk without giving her any hope, or taking it away. She went to church every day to pray for his return, or his safety, at least. She had a feeling he was still alive and didn't want anyone to rob her of that feeling. "Close the door and don't be afraid. I'll be back before you open your eyes. If I'm late don't worry. I won't be long. Just a few days and I'll be back." She never forgot that sentence.

She would close her eyes and open them again, searching for Tamim, waiting for a miracle that never materialized. Um Tamim, as she liked to be called, refused to lock the door with a key when she slept or went out. "What if he comes back, how would he come in?" Her husband would respond, "How can he come back? They don't allow anyone to return. God knows if he's still alive anyway. He would've at least contacted us by now." When she heard that, her tears would flow. She couldn't believe that he lost all hope, and wanted to kill the hope she still had. Hope dies last. Even after she and his father both died, the front door was never locked.

"Do you know what it means to spend your life waiting? Waiting for those who left to return? You wait your whole life and keep talking about the past. But the past grows bigger and devours you. An entire people, those who stayed, seem mad when they talk about all that was before. As if what was wasn't, or it was a world that only existed in their imagination. Jaffa. Jaffa is a name that pains me. I curse it every day, because I still love it. Can you spit at what you love? Yes, because this love kills you. Look at our situation. The drugs, poverty, and disgust. Just look. Staying here means bleeding and living with an open and gushing wound, but you keep on living. How can I explain what I feel? I feel happy that I stayed, despite the misery, pain, and forgetfulness. Yes, forgetfulness. No one understands. No one understands our disaster, but they all exploit it. No one realizes the extent of the loneliness those of us who stayed here feel. My father was right when he said that tears have dried up. Our tears have dried up."

This is what Yusif once said to David after an argument they had about politics. He said it all angrily, and in Hebrew.

David remembered that today while he was waiting for the bus. Sunlight had made its way in the sky, driving away the darkness. He looked at his watch. It was odd that the no. 10 bus he took from Jaffa to Tel Aviv was forty-five minutes late. A crowd had gathered around and people were grumbling.

Yusif was the one who usually drove that bus. He started his shift early in the morning. David took a deep puff from his cigarette, as if it were an oxygen tube, and then threw the stump on the asphalt. Had he walked, he could've reached the center of Tel Aviv and taken a bus to work from there. Why were the buses late? Why was Yusif late? When the bus finally arrived, it was packed with passengers who resembled fish cramped in a sardine can. Three of them got off. Some of those waiting, including David, rushed to catch it. But it drove away, puffing its exhaust smoke in their faces and showing them its backend. There was an ad featuring a blond woman trying to hold down her white dress in the wind, à la Marilyn Monroe. Those chasing the bus looked at her red lips as both she and the bus moved away.

"He's a fucking son of a bitch," said a tall thin man to David.

"Yusif must be sick. I know him. He would never be late or miss work unless it's an emergency."

The man didn't appear to understand what David meant. The number of passengers waiting at the bus stop increased as did their complaints. Taxis and buses full of passengers drove by, but they didn't stop. After more than an hour, an almost empty bus stopped. Those still waiting got on quickly and heaped their anger at the driver. "What the hell is this? Are we in the third world?" "Only in this country do buses run away from passengers." "You should be ashamed of yourselves. What kind of service is this?" The driver absorbed their anger with his silence and nods, indicating that he understood their complaints. David went up to him to ask about what was going on.

"The Arabs have declared war and are on strike today."

"That's impossible. Why didn't we hear anything about a strike on the news? I have a lot of Arab friends and none of them said anything. I would've known."

"What? Are you their legal adviser or something? Anyway, excuse me, sir, I have to pay attention to the road."

David stood there, holding on to the iron bar in the middle of the bus, looking at the street as the bus drowned in chatter and prognostications. Meanwhile, the phones at the Dan and Egged companies were ringing nonstop, with variations on one question: Why were the buses late? Both companies instructed their customer support employees to stick to the following message in answering all queries:

"We apologize for the delay. We have no information as to why Arab drivers did not report to work today. We have no knowledge of any strike. We will try to resolve the issue as soon as possible. We would like to assure you that this will not affect traffic today, because we have recalled Jewish drivers who were on vacation. We ask for your patience. The country is going through a difficult time. Thank you for your understanding."

7

Prison 48

Rafi's white face was now the color of turnip. His eyes bulged and his jaw dropped when he opened the gate to cell number 5. He wouldn't have been that shocked even if he'd seen the corpse of a prisoner who had committed suicide, or died of torture. He's been at it for thirty years, and his skin is thicker than a crocodile's, as he often said, sarcastically. He has no feelings toward the terrorists. That's what he used to call them. He might pity them at times, especially the young ones.

He called out "prisoner number 3" into the silence of the cold cell. The silence didn't respond. He peered inside carefully while holding the gate with his right hand. He called out again, with an anxious voice, for prisoner number 3 to come out and stand in line for the 6 a.m. count. Holding his nose to avoid the stench, he stepped into the cell. He stood perplexed in the middle, looking at the walls. As if searching for an ant or a roach, or something hiding in there, but not for Waleed. He began to sweat, felt his temperature rise, and could hear his heart pounding. He looked at the lock, looked for a hole in the wall through which Waleed might have escaped. The guard was now trapped in the cell.

He barked into his walkie-talkie, "Prisoner number 3 is not in his cell. Repeat. Prisoner 3 not in cell 5." Other voices yelling in disbelief numbers and similar phrases followed from empty cells and wards in prison number 48.

Menachem was on his way to that prison, which was about seventy kilometers north of the White City. There was no sign indicating its existence. Those who drove on Route 4 to Haifa wondered about the side road branching off. There was no sign, not even one of those indicating a restricted military area. Nothing but pines and cypresses through which some dim lights could be seen.

Menachem was driving his old Mercedes without paying much attention to road signs. He knew the road by heart. There were dark patches under his eyes carrying his fatigue.

"Why doesn't this bastard just die and give me a break? These idiots hit him like he's some doll. I can't believe that I haven't finished my article. All because they use excessive force and then call me thinking he's about to die. He didn't die yesterday, nor the day before. I told Rafi to give him a break for a day. Let him sleep. He stinks. They didn't allow him to go to the toilet. They call me for the third night in a row. As if mercy suddenly found a place in their hearts and they can't wait for me to come for my usual appointment. When I got there yesterday he was frothing and it was disgusting. How old is prisoner number 3? Seventeen? I don't know why I'm possessed by this one. Perhaps because he is standing between me and finishing the article. Miri! Do you hear me? Are you still there?"

Because of the time difference and being occupied with an article about humane torture for a famous British magazine, this was the only time in the last few days that he was able to talk to his daughter, who was studying in New York.

"Yes, Aba. OK. But you know I have problems with you working as a doctor with political prisoners. A torture doctor. We've argued a lot about it and I don't want us to talk now, while you're driving."

"Were it not for me, some of them wouldn't be alive. Do you know that? I try to make prison conditions for these terrorists humane. I told Rafi that that young man will not withstand the shaking and he should stop using that technique, but he won't. Even if you try it with eight thousand of them, and it works, this one won't withstand it. Rabin asked once in a radio interview why the Shabak should stop using this method if it worked with so many. This young man won't survive, even if thousands before him did. I told them so. I always warn them not to use inhumane methods in torture. That's why my presence there is important. You know that!"

There was only the occasional "hmmm" and some tense breathing on the other side.

"Are you still there, sweetie?"

"Yes, yes. And what did he say when you told him that torture won't work with that prisoner?"

"We'll shove a stick up his ass. That's exactly what Rafi said. Sorry for the language, but I just want you to realize that I have to be there. It would've been much worse if I hadn't been there. This time Rafi sounded like he was dead serious about doing exactly that to number 3. I know you have some Arab friends and you're against all these measures. I'm with you, but am not sure we have any other option."

"Ok, Aba."

"Oh, sweetie. I am there and I have to hang up now. You know the security precautions. I'll call you from home tomorrow. OK?"

"OK. Bye."

"Bye. Take care."

Once he got to the huge black iron gate, Menachem stopped the car engine as was required. He got out and went to the scanner where his face and palm were identified. He went back and turned the ignition again and waited for the black gate to be opened. The building's courtyard was full of pines and cypresses. There were some rose bushes near the wooden benches, where prison staff sat down to sip coffee or smoke during breaks between torture sessions. Nothing in the courtyard indicated the nature of what took place inside. Everything looked clean and calm from the bench. The building, like the prisoners themselves, had no official existence. Neither the guards nor the prisoners existed. What mattered was extracting information. Whoever is sent to prison 48 must be a dangerous target. Those who make the decisions to send them here know what they're doing.

Menachem parked his car in the space designated for doctors. As per instructions, he left all electronics inside the car. When he got to the prison clinic he found Rafi lying on a bed waiting for him. He was sweating profusely and screaming of severe stomach pain. Menachem fought a smile and thought, for a moment, that prisoner 3 had assaulted Rafi and injured him.

"What happened?"

"The son of a bitch disappeared. When I catch him I'm going to tear him to pieces. They've all disappeared. I'll tear them to pieces when I catch them. They won't get away from us!"

8

Hospital

"Get up Habiba! I have to bathe you."

"Where is the doctor? I'm tired."

"He hasn't come yet. Get up so you can bathe before he arrives. Your surgery is in an hour."

"What time is it now? I feel very tired. Maybe it's better to postpone the surgery . . ."

"It's seven. Don't worry. Dr. Shanneer is the best in all of Sharon. He graduated from America. Come on, let's go."

The nurse said the last phrase decisively to convince Habiba to get up before her daughter comes.

Most people calculate their age the way we measure the age of trees. Each ring counts for a year. But Habiba, who was in her seventies, used to say that she was fifteen. The years had left their traces on her face. She had made the long journey from Baghdad to Hatikva in "Tal al-Khirbe," (The Hill of Ruins) as she insisted on calling Tel Aviv, which she never liked. She hated the humidity and the stinky caravans where those who came from Arab countries were housed. They lived in poor and miserable dwellings. The Tel

Aviv municipality refused to incorporate the neighborhood even fifteen years after the establishment of Azrael (that's what she used to call the state). She kept speaking Arabic to her parents and her children too. But her grandchildren mimic the Ashkenazis in their habits and lifestyle. That broke her heart. They were ashamed of their Arab origin and would insult Arabs a lot. Her mother called European Jews "Polish" and often said they were not real Jews, because their habits and ways were so alien to her. She would mention the wounding looks that inspected her and sprayed her with DDT after their airplane had landed in the airport when they arrived. They sprayed them like cattle being inoculated before being herded to a farm.

Her body aged, but the fifteen-year-old girl stayed inside. Habiba preferred that her daughter bathe her and not the nurse. She didn't like hospitals. It was at a hospital where she first tasted separation when her husband died of cancer, twenty years after her arrival in Palestine. After that she only went to hospitals to visit mothers who had just given birth. That as a sign of good omen and a new beginning.

She bathed and went back to her room with the nurse to find her daughter waiting with a smile. The nurse helped her put on a blue robe. Her daughter combed her long hair and braided it. Habiba often told her how her hair used to be long and thicker than wool, but today it's like a silk thread. She waited calmly for the doctor. The nurse disappeared and returned

half an hour later to say that he hadn't come. Habiba
was anxious, especially that she hated surgeries. Were
it not that Dr. Aziz Shanneer had come himself and
reassured her, explaining in detail what he was going
to do to her cartilage, she wouldn't have agreed to
have surgery at this age. She was on the threshold of
her grave, as she used to say. He asked her how she
knew that she wouldn't live another twenty years? So
why live them in pain when she can have a surgery
with a very high rate of success. He made sure to look
her in the eye as he said, in Arabic, "You'll be as good
as a new bride. Not like today's spoiled girls."

She laughed to overcome her embarrassment.
She told her daughter that he looked like her father:
tall with honey-colored eyes that change their color.
Aziz laughed and said in Arabic, "Hopefully, everything will be fine, *Hajja*." She liked "*Hajja*," which
she hadn't heard in a long time. She smiled, because
Arabic was the language of the heart and of sweet
memories.

Habiba lied down waiting in her bed looking at
the clear morning sky through the window. Her hair
smelled like apples. She used to take her own shampoo along wherever she went. She feared that after
all these years she couldn't remember exactly what
her late husband's eyes looked like. So she asked her
daughter to hand her his photograph from the inlaid
wooden box. She'd put her most cherished items
there. Some she had brought from Baghdad, others

she collected here in Palestine. There were many family photographs, including one of her as a bride of eighteen next to her husband. Everyone in those photographs, except her, had died. There was a braid of her mother's hair and a small pouch containing dirt from the garden of their Baghdad house. Her wedding ring, which became too tight after she gave birth to her second child, was in it too.

She opened the box and took her husband's photograph out. It was taken one year before his death. She touched his face and eyes with her fingertips and placed her hand on her hair as if retracing his own touch. Then she asked her daughter to call the nurse to see what was going on.

"I don't know why the doctor is late. He's not answering his phone. Just wait. We'll see what we can do. I will come back later."

The nurse said, and sighed indicating her impatience with these repeated inquiries. Then she added:

"There is news that the Arabs in Israel, and Judea and Samaria, are on strike, but it is yet to be confirmed."

"I don't understand."

"What is not clear about what I said?"

"Are the doctors on strike?

"No, just the Arabs, it seems."

Habiba heard her stomach growling. She was told to fast before the surgery. She went back to gaze at the clear sky outside her window. The nurse came back later to tell them that the surgery was postponed, and they would be informed later of the new date. Habiba looked at her daughter and said, in a shaky voice tinged with disappointment, "Let's eat."

9

A Building

Rothschild Boulevard bounced back to life and its commotion began to seep into the apartments in building 5A. They responded in kind. The sounds of radios and TV screens escaped from under the doors, or through open windows, and sank into the noise on the street.

The man with fluffy white hair was wearing a black undershirt and a white pair of boxers. He started listening to music on his radio with excessive joy, as if for the first time. He picked up a bag of Italian coffee and smelled its aroma. He filled one big spoon and fed it to the espresso machine. After adding water, he stood there waiting and admiring the machine. His wife used to mock him whenever she saw him in this state. "It's as if you're looking at a Mercedes," she used to mumble. But she wasn't there this morning. She had left the day before to visit her family in Jerusalem. He didn't like her family or Jerusalem. They were religious and kept Shabbat and he doesn't. His wife stopped observing Shabbat, but she only cooks and eats kosher and her family keeps pressuring him to pray and keep kosher.

This morning he doesn't have to answer her questions, or engage in meaningless conversations about her relatives and friends. He won't hear her calling him from the kitchen telling him to answer the phone, something he doesn't like to. Why else was the answering machine invented? Whoever wants to talk to him can leave him a message and he'll get back to them later. He refused to buy a cell phone despite all the fights they had about the subject.

He stretched out lazily on the bamboo rocking chair in the living room. Sipping his coffee and listening to the radio in peace reminds him of his mornings back when he was single and lived alone. He sipped his espresso as he listened to the news.

Meanwhile, the woman who lived right above him was wiping away her tears. Following a long night, agonizing over a recent breakup, she got out of bed and took off the clothes she'd had slept in. She turned on the TV so as not to feel lonely, and stood naked in front of the mirror, looking for the ghost of a wrinkle on her face. She walked to the kitchen to quench her thirst, looking at every mirror she passed by, the apartment was full them, as if to console herself with her young body, which so many men told her was so dazzling.

A few drops of the water she was drinking trickled down all the way to her breasts. She went back to her bedroom and raised the TV's volume. She looked into the mirror again and touched her face. She wasn't paying attention to the chatter on "Good Morning Israel" at first. But she ignored her reflection in the mirror and sat on the edge of her bed gazing at the TV screen in disbelief.

At that exact moment, another neighbor of hers, on the second floor, was cursing *Haaretz*, because the delivery person was late. It wasn't the first time the bastard was late and, without the paper, his morning will not be the same. He sat in his balcony, just as he did at that time every morning. A plate with three pieces of whole wheat bread and another with butter cubes and the apple jam he made himself, and a cup of American coffee, sat on the table. He usually ate his breakfast while reading the newspaper. Classical music, mostly Chopin, but sometimes Rachmaninoff, could be heard in the background.

But instead of reading the newspaper, he was listening to the radio, and looking at the public bus, which had stopped in front of the building. It stood there puffing its black smoke in the face of the morning. The bus driver raised the volume of the radio when the announcer noted that it was the eight o'clock news bulletin. The AC was out of order and most of the windows were open. The news pierced the ears of pedestrians.

"It's eight in the morning. I am Tamar Netanyahu and this is the news bulletin:

A state of maximum emergency was declared in the country because the Arabs have declared a general strike. Security and police units have recalled reserves. All of the Arab inhabitants of Israel, Judea and Samaria, and Gaza have disappeared. All Arab prisoners in civil and military prisons have disappeared, including those with blood on their hands. Prison authorities and police, as well as the IDF, are investigating the matter and coordinating their efforts. Business owners have reported that their Arab employees did not show up to their jobs. The government is holding an emergency session with the chiefs of military and security to discuss the matter. The prime minister has consulted with regional and western leaders. It is expected that the government spokesperson will hold a press conference in the coming few hours.

Earlier this morning, police summoned the heads of sects, Arab tribes, as well as heads of municipalities and local councils to register at the nearest police stations.

The police have set up mobile checkpoints at the entrances of Arab cities and villages in Israel. Security has been tightened as well on all cross-points with Judea and Samaria. The minister of defense declared the latter closed military areas. Arab areas in mixed cities are under surveillance to ensure no exit or entry. The police instructed citizens to be vigilant and to report any information or suspicious movements they might notice.

It is worth noting that neither the Arab leaders in Israel, nor the Palestinian Authority, had declared their intention to stage a strike. Security officials are scanning and analyzing all the footage from surveillance cameras in public places. No official response from the state has been issued as of now. Finally, here is the weather forecast: Sunny with temperatures reaching 20 degrees Celsius. This was a news summary prepared by Tamar Netanyahu.

We are changing our normal schedule and will have special coverage of the disappearance of the Arabs so as to keep you posted about the latest developments. Our guest in the studio today is Shlomo Ben Gaon, an expert on Arab affairs."

When the bus started moving, the angry man was relieved. The engine's noise had disrupted the serenity of his morning hours. He called the public relations office at *Haaretz* to complain about the newspaper not being delivered, and to ask for a refund. It wasn't the first time. He then put on a blue shirt, grey pants, and sandals over the soft black socks he always wore, even in summer. He slammed the door behind him and walked to the kiosk near his house to buy the paper.

10

Ariel

Ariel dragged himself out of bed and went to the kitchen. He wanted to sleep some more, but couldn't. Books and newspapers were scattered everywhere in the living room. He had to tidy up.

It took seven steps to get to the little kitchen. He opened the big silver refrigerator and stood there perplexed, as if he'd forgotten that he came to drink water. He took a bite out of a red apple that sat on one of the shelves. He had brushed his teeth before going to sleep, but the sour taste of wine from the night before lingered. Maybe the apple will change that.

He should take a shower, he thought, as he scratched his head. He put the apple on the tiny kitchen table. He went to the bathroom, jumped under the shower, and thought about his ten-day vacation. He has to buy a few things for his apartment, including a new bath mat. As he scrubbed his body under the hot water, he heard an impulsive door ring. It was rare for anyone to come without calling beforehand. Maybe it's by mistake, or the mailman. The ringing didn't stop and it was joined by knocks and banging on the door. He shut the water, took a towel, and wrapped it hastily around his waist. He went and opened the door without even asking who it was, or looking through the peephole.

It was his ex, Zohar, but he didn't recognize her at first. She had cut her coal-black hair short and died it a light chestnut color that didn't suit her.

"Shalom. Why did it take you forever to open the door? And why are you still asleep when there is such a big mess in the country?"

"I didn't know that you are an investigator now. What are you talking about? What mess? Was there a terrorist attack?"

He asked her to come in. He hadn't seen her since they broke up. It was strange for her to visit. Maybe it was one of her crazy fits and she wants to get back together. As he closed the door, he heard her weeping. He'd never seen so much fear in her eyes. He took her in his arms.

"We're finished. They'll finish us off."

"Who will be finished?"

"Didn't you hear the news? The Palestinians have disappeared without a trace. Neither here nor in Judea and Samaria. I don't know if we did it ourselves, somehow, or if they're hiding somewhere. Either way, Arab countries will attack us and tear us to pieces."

Ariel laughed.

"You're hallucinating. Did you drink something last night, or is it a new kid of hash? I want some too."

She wiped away her tears and pushed him aside.

"Don't make light of the situation. It's not a joke. Didn't you hear the news?"

He picked up the remote, turned the radio on, and scanned it looking for the Army Radio Station. He turned the TV on, too, but kept it on mute. The announcer was reminding listeners that the Palestinians have disappeared.

Ariel was incredulous.

"What are they talking about? I don't understand."

"The Arabs are gone! Simply gone. None of them showed up to work. Their houses are empty and their phones ring, but no one answers. The workers, beggars, prisoners, teachers, patients, café owners, cooks, and garbage men. They are aaaaaaaaaall gonnnnnneeeee."

She took a deep breath and continued.

"No one knows what is happening. They disappeared, Ariel. *Na'lamu ata mifen zeh na'lamuuuuu*?"

"Calm down please. You're losing it. I've never seen you like this."

"What about your Arab friends? They didn't tell you about it?"

"I was with Alaa last night until around eleven, or shortly thereafter. We talked a bit and then he went to his apartment. Wait, I'll call him and you'll see for yourself." Ariel went to the bedroom and put on black underpants and a pair of jeans, and a white V-neck T-shirt. He came back with his cell phone in hand and dialed Alaa's number. Zohar sat on the couch looking out the window to her left.

"His phone is turned off, or out of coverage. He's supposed to be at work now. We came back relatively early so he could get up in time for work."

"You don't get it, do you? All the Palestinians have disappeared. You won't find Alaa, or the others. I don't care about them. But we need to know where they went and what is happening?"

"I'll go knock on his door. Wait here!"

He went out barefoot and ran down to the third floor. He rang Alaa's bell, confident that he'd open the door in no time, if he's not at work. Taking time to open the door doesn't mean anything necessarily. Alaa's usually late. Ariel rang the bell several times and then started banging on the door and calling out, "Alaa, Alaa, *ata bu?*"

When he went back up Zohar was getting ready to leave.

"He's not answering."

"You mean he *disappeared* with the others."

"I don't want to get into an argument, but I don't think he's disappeared. Maybe he's wiped out and wasn't able to go to work. We drank a whole bottle of wine last night and he was tired. His phone is off and he only turns it off when he's asleep."

"You still don't get what's happening. Listen to your voicemail. Listen to the news. This is the nonchalant attitude that ruined our relationship. I'm going."

He asked her to stay, but she was determined to leave. He checked his voicemail.

"Ariel, it's your mother. Please call me back as soon as you get this."

"Ariel, mother here again. Call me! Where are you? Why is your phone turned off? I'm very worried about you. Please call."

"Hi Ariel, Matthew here. I'm sure you've already heard. I know you are on vacation, but this is an emergency. Call us right away. We sent several e-mails. Please call ASAP."

"Shalom Ariel. This is Dany. I returned two days ago and I'd planned to call you earlier to have a drink, but am calling now because of what happened. Maybe you have some information or explanation? Please call me."

"Ariel, this is Zohar. Please call me."

"Zohar again. I'll stop by your place, maybe you're there. I'm worried about you. Call me."

He felt numb. He couldn't believe what was happening. As if it's doomsday. Is it a war? He called Alaa again. No answer. He didn't even reach his voicemail so he could say a sentence or two in the hopes that Alaa would call back once he hears the message. All he got was the automatic message: "The number you called is outside the service area. Please try again later."

He called his mother, who said in a shaky voice:

"Where are you? I've been trying to get a hold of you since this morning. I'm very worried. I miss your father. Were he alive we'd know what is happening."

"How about good morning first, mother? Please calm down. No need to worry this much. Everything will be fine. Had there been any danger, we would've known right away. Please calm down."

"But the news is worrisome. It reminds me of Yom Kippur, when the Arabs attacked us from all sides, and we were going to lose everything. Do you understand what I'm saying?"

"There is no need for all this, please. What you're saying isn't true. We defeated them in just six days and regained our strength. No need to worry. I'll call Dod Itzik and get back to you, please."

"Ok, I'll wait for your call."

He liked to call him "Dod Itzik," "Uncle Itzik," as if the two went together. His affection and respect for Itzik increased after his father died. They remained close even if and when they disagreed. Ariel did not think it was necessary to keep the West Bank and Gaza. That's what he called them at times. Otherwise it's always "Judea and Samaria." During his reserve military service, he was sent to Hebron. That was his nightmare. He thought about refusing to go there, but he decided that his presence and writing about it would be more important and consequential than refusing to serve. He wrote about it and some stopped talking to him after that. Alaa used to tell Ariel that he was merely creating "good" excuses to justify horrors. Itzik used to criticize him a lot, too, but for other reasons. But Itzik stood by his side and never

abandoned him. Perhaps because he had paternal feelings toward him. There was an argument about the
country's priorities during the last dinner where he
and Itzik were guests. Ariel said that Iran was Israel's
major problem and they had to focus on Hizballah,
because it is its long arm in Lebanon. They should
withdraw from the West Bank and Gaza and allow
for the establishment of a demilitarized Palestinian
state. Those seated around the table were aghast and
looked at him as if he'd just arrived from outer space.
They were all were in agreement about Iran, but they
objected to the idea and location of a demilitarized
state. For how could Ariel, the son of an IDF hero,
utter such words? His father was killed when his heli-
copter crashed during a military operation in south
Lebanon. How could he call Judea and Samaria "the
West Bank and Gaza?" How could he say that they
don't need them, and that a Palestinian entity must be
established there and they should swap the land and
settlements? Spitting in their faces would've been less
offensive. Itzik interceded and took care of remedying
the situation. The subject was closed and it was only
revisited later when Itzik called to talk to him. The
other guests were so appalled by Ariel's statement. It
didn't matter to them that he was not against military service in principle. He just didn't think it was
useful to serve in the territories to provide protection
for settlements.

Ariel went to the bathroom to take a leak. His
phone was in his hand and he dialed Itzik's number.

He looked in the long mirror. It was a strange moment. He thought his face belonged to some other person whom he'd met, but didn't know very well. Itzik wasn't answering. He put the phone aside, washed his hands quickly, and then went back to the living room to call others.

11

Ariel

Dear Matthew,

I tried calling you, but you were not at the office. I heard the voicemail you left. Since I was on break today, I didn't keep my cell on and I overslept. I only woke up because I was so thirsty (too much wine last night!). What is happening in the country is *Tohu va vohu*. I called one of my father's old friends many times and finally got a hold of him. His answer to my inquiries was shocking. He said that no one knows exactly what happened.

He occupies a sensitive position, so if he doesn't know what is taking place, then our situation is quite dangerous, unless we solve this conundrum in the next forty-eight hours. *Tohu va vohu*! No one, and I stress, no one, knows what the hell is going on. I'll file my article in the next few hours.

More later
Shalom Ovrakha
Ariel

12

Ariel

"Dear Listeners, we continue our special coverage. It is ten past eleven a.m. and we have Shlomo Ben Gaon, expert on Arab affairs, with us here in the studio. We will try to answer your questions and comments, and will be taking calls for the next two hours. Hagit, from Jerusalem, is on the line. Hagit, *Shalom Ovrakha*, go ahead."

"Shalom everybody! All these media outlets are saying it's too early to say for sure what has happened. *Aval eluhim yashmour.* I can't understand how it's almost midday and our government has yet to issue a statement clarifying what is going on. The media has been repeating the same line since the early morning. 'We don't know what is happening.' How can we not know what is happening? Where are the surveillance cameras? Is what you announced about security detainees having disappeared true? If so, then we will face an army of terrorists who will come out of nowhere. An army of thousands who are trained to kill and wreak havoc. Can the IDF control them? They are ticking bombs, ready to blow themselves

63

up. What will happen if thousands of Arabs blow themselves up in our midst? Are we ready for this scenario?"

"Oh oh, Hagit, *tiragai ktsat*. Relax! We don't want to terrify our listeners. You should be more careful with these wild prognostications that stem for an understandable, but rather exaggerated fear. Ben Gaon, could you comment on what Hagit said?"

"There is, undoubtedly, a general state of fear, but we have to remember that we are still in control. That the IDF or the government have not declared an official response until now, doesn't necessarily mean they don't have information about this matter. The confusion in the media doesn't necessarily reflect any confusion or threat on the security level. What is taking place is a storm, a powerful one, or one that appears to be powerful. But it should not make us lose our self-confidence, or our confidence in our army. We, and our allies, are the strongest in the world, and no one can touch us. This doesn't mean that the terrorists will not try to do something to weaken our morale. There is no doubt that we are facing a number of issues that are still unclear. There is also a feeling of disappointment in regards to Israeli Arabs. We have trusted them to live together with us in peace and try to coexist without them trying to destroy us. At any rate, we must preserve our unity. We are still waiting for reactions from Arab states which haven't issued any official statements against us so far. Some of the so-called Arab Spring states are waging a propaganda campaign against us and inciting people, but we are used to that. What is important is to be vigilant and careful."

"Thank you Hagit. We'll take another caller. Daniel, from Netanya. How are you Daniel?"

"I'm doing great. I'm so happy."

"Oh, I'm happy that someone is happy, and doesn't seem to be worried. Tell us why you are so happy?"

"The news we've been hearing since this morning is great. I would like to salute our brave soldiers who carried out a clean operation to rid us of the fifth column and terrorists who were around us everywhere. We have finally cleaned up the country and achieved what we weren't able to do during the war of independence. But what I still don't understand is all this fear and noise about the Arabs disappearing, or being deported by the IDF? As far as I'm concerned, this was a problem that we finally managed to solve. Does it matter how? The friends of Arabs, or let us say, the friends of the Palestinians, because our state has no qualms with Arabs in neighboring countries, except for Hizballah and Iran. Anyway, the friends of terrorists who are now screaming and wondering where their friends are. To these leftists I say, if you love Arabs so much, just go with them wherever they have gone. Let them establish a state where al-Qaida is, or anywhere. Look, even Arabs don't want these terrorists. Everyone wants to keep them here and to send those ticking bombs from refugee camps here.

I don't like these two-faced leftists. Why worry and waste time talking about where and how the Arabs disappeared? What's important is that they're gone. It doesn't matter how. Let them go to hell, or to Arab countries. I think our brave army is responsible for this genius operation, which will go down in history . . ."

"*Toda Raba* Daniel. Ben Gaon?"

"Daniel's approach is important. He doesn't want to stir and spread fear in the country, and is trying to maintain confidence. But we shouldn't exaggerate, of course. We must be very careful not to say that the IDF is responsible for what happened to the Arabs. We must remember that, as of yet, we don't know for sure what is taking place. More importantly, Israel is a state of laws and is still the only democracy in the region. The Muslim Brotherhood, who were brought about by the Arab Spring, have produced Salafis and sharia states, not secular democracies like ours. We are a country of laws. We represent western values and civilization in the midst of these backward states. The doors will, for sure, be open now for bilateral relations and peace agreements. Daniel is correct in that even the Arabs are tired of Palestinians. So, *yalla basta*. Whether the Arabs went by choice or they were planning a massive suicide mission, it is crucial for things to be clear and ethical and to proceed according to the law. If the disappearance continues, there is no doubt that many problems will be solved. But we have to be steadfast, wait, and be vigilant."

"Apologies, Ben Gaon, I have to interrupt you. Tamer Weiss, our correspondent in Tel Aviv is on the line from Dizengoff Street. Tamer, how are things?"

"Dorit, we are in the middle of Tel Aviv. Streets are less crowded than usual at this hour of the day. Pedestrian movement and traffic were normal earlier in the morning, but have slowed down now. I spoke to some shop owners, particularly those who sell food in and outside Dizengoff Mall. These are usually packed with customers around noon. Many restaurant owners confirmed that traffic was slower compared to previous days, but it wasn't affected too much since those who come here work in the area. But the stores depend on shoppers, many of whom preferred to stay home, follow the news, and be careful, especially that the news about the disappearance has been confirmed. But even if restaurant owners are correct, car traffic in Dizengoff is still semi-normal for this time of day. At any rate, Tel Aviv is always teeming with life and no one can stop it. Back to you, Dorit."

"Tamer, did you canvass voices on the street? Did the police announce any new measures that citizens must follow?"

"Dorit, we spoke to many pedestrians as well as store owners. The great majority of them don't seem to be too worried. There is vigilance, but I think the strong presence of police and security throughout the country is reassuring. The police have increased their presence in the city center, especially here on

Dizengoff and in the surrounding area. They have
called on citizens to be careful and continue with their
lives as usual, but be vigilant. According to one police
official we spoke to, due to the anxiety some are feeling, calls informing on items thought to be bombs or
explosives are five times the normal rate. The police
take each call seriously and follow up. However, they
haven't found anything dangerous until now. Back to
you in the studio, Dorit."

"Thank you, Tamer. This was Tamer Weiss who
gave us an idea about the atmosphere on Dizengoff
Street in Tel Aviv. There will be a summary of the
news very soon and we will continue afterward with
some analysis from our guest in the studio in the next
hour. We will continue to take your calls and listen to
your opinions, and will hear from our correspondents
in Tel Aviv, Jerusalem, Haifa, the north and south, as
well as Kiryat Arba, and other points. It is midday.
We'll be back after the news."

к

Ariel turned down the volume on the radio to a background whisper, and turned up the TV. He surfed
through channels and settled on the special coverage
on Channel 2. He browsed some international and
Israeli newspaper sites on his laptop. He turned up
the volume some more to be able to hear it in the
kitchen where he went next to make some coffee.
The news mentioned that all areas where Palestinians resided had been declared closed military zones.

Several journalists said in interviews that they had tried to enter these areas, including Jaffa, but the army prevented them from doing so.

Press offices refused to give any special entry permits to those areas during the coming forty-eight hours. Going there would be of no use anyway, he thought as he took a sip of the coffee, which scorched his tongue. He called the IDF press office and the Tel Aviv municipality to check if it was necessary to get a special permit to go to Jaffa, or any other Arab area. He got the same answer. No permits are being given and he should call the following day.

13

Sahtayn Hummus

Sahtayn had been open for ten years. Its owners, Akram and his wife Yasmeen, have excellent rapport with their customers. They often forget that the two are Palestinians except when they hear them speaking Arabic to each other, or to one of their children.

Roni comes all the way from north Tel Aviv once a week just to eat at Sahtayn. After finishing his breakfast there, he usually walks the ten steps from Sahtayn Hummus to Café Sarah, nearby on Shenkin Street, to drink his coffee and read the newspaper.

Today, however, there was no confident smile, political joke, or a curse about the rising cost of life in Tel Aviv. Nor were there complaints, questions, sighs, or any new Arabic words for Roni to learn. Sahtayn was closed and many of its customers went back after standing in front of its dirt-colored, iron door. There was no sign posted to indicate that it would be closed today.

Roni's walk from Sahtayn to Café Sarah was lonely and slower than usual. "We won't forget, nor forgive the fifth of November, 1995" read the slogan on one of tens of posters that covered the glass facade of Café Sara. Roni used to stop and read the writing on all the posters every time he entered the café. This ritual reassured him that things were still the same since the last time he came the week before.

He didn't exchange greetings and niceties with Sara this time. He just said *"Boker"* but without *"tov."* He didn't tell her how delicious the hummus at Akram and Yasmeen's was. They usually chat as he reads his newspaper, cursing the Israeli right and lamenting the days of Rabin. Had Rabin lived, everything would have been better. Sara and Roni agree on that every week. But this week he had many questions for which Sara had no answer. Sara wasn't herself either. She didn't crack any jokes, or regale him with one of her many stories. She looked at her watch and was surprised that he had come at that hour.

"What happened? Why are you here early? You usually come in the late afternoon. It's twelve thirty now."

"Did you see Akram and Yasmeen?"

"Yeah, they each drank their coffee here during their break yesterday. Akram came back after closing the shop and stayed here for a while. He smoked more than usual and was absent-minded. When I asked him about it, his eyes welled up, and he said he was ill. He has kidney problems and doesn't know what to do. He was thinking of Yasmeen and their children. He was going to start treatment next week and had to talk to Yasmeen. He hadn't told her yet.

Then he kissed me on the cheek and left saying 'till tomorrow.' He walked slowly though."

"Do you think that's why the shop is closed?"

"I don't know. Maybe something bigger. They say the Palestinians are on strike today!"

"Strike? Why would they go on strike?"

"Didn't you hear the news? They are saying they want to improve their conditions."

"Buy why go on strike? What does improving their conditions mean? Who's stopping them from that?"

"What can I say?"

"I don't get this nonsense. Why would they go on strike? What do they lack? I don't care, but they should've announced it beforehand. I'll take my coffee to go today. I won't be drinking it here."

Sara shrugged and didn't say anything. Roni left and stammered as he bid her farewell. He left Shenkin and its busy cafes, small shops, and the noise of tourists, and headed to Allenby Street. He passed by some tiny shops and thought they were whispering to each other, conspiring against him, and hiding the secret behind the disappearance of Sahtayn's owners.

14

Airport

Clouds were absent at that hour. The sun took its place, alone, amid the sky of that tiny country. It resembled a big sesame seed. Blood-red dominated the information screens for departing and arriving flights. All flights had been cancelled for the next twenty-four hours. Most understood that, because the country was witnessing an unspecified danger. Therefore, unity in the ranks and the house was necessary. This is what many had said, and what the media had been trying to relay since early morning. But a few travelers were furious about these measures and could not understand the need for them. Nor did they understand the correlation between the strike of the Palestinians, or their disappearance, as some said, and halting all air traffic. People appeared lost in the airport, which was usually a place of utmost order and control.

A traveler who had not acclimated to the country, even after living in it for five years, and who was sick of the strange logic of things, said, "What is odd about Arabs not showing up for work or going on strike? They don't work at the airport anyway, so why would air traffic be affected by their presence or absence?"

He yelled at the woman standing behind the information desk.

"Why should I care if the Arabs didn't show up to work, or if they have disappeared? Let them go to hell all together. Why should we give a fuck?"

The Frenchman stopped yelling and waited for an answer, but she just raised her eyebrows:

"I'm sorry. I don't have any further information."

"Why do they delay travel and what is this strike? Why would they go on strike? If they don't like it here, they can go to Arab countries. They have more than twenty of them."

The woman shook her head again and smiled. The cranky Frenchman stood there, shaking his head too, and then snarled and followed that with a deep sigh. The waiting went on. Many lost any hope of the travel ban being lifted. It appeared that it would go on for more than twenty-four hours. So, they left the airport and returned to where they had come from. Herds of humans, all walking in one direction.

15

Ariel

Sometimes, taking a walk helps him find new ideas. He put on his elegant Geo sneakers. There were a few specks of dirt stuck to the sole of his left sneaker, so he kicked them off with his right sole.

He put his wallet in his back pocket, his cell phone in the front pocket, and headed to the door. He stood before the key hanger next to the door. He was about to take his apartment key when he glimpsed the key to Alaa's apartment dangling from the adjacent hook. They had exchanged spare keys in case one of them lost his. He clinched it anxiously and went up to Alaa's apartment on the third floor.

He rang the doorbell, then banged on the door. He didn't wait long and just took Alaa's key out, and turned it, nervously, inside the lock. He hesitated a bit in his first few steps inside the apartment. What if Alaa was inside? He'll understand why Ariel is doing this, he told himself.

"Alaa! Alaa. *Ata bu?*"

His voice searched timidly inside the apartment for Alaa.

"Alaa! *Ata bu? Ze ani*, Ariel."

The aroma of the cardamom Alaa used to put in his coffee hit him as soon as he entered. He must've had his last cup a few hours before, otherwise the aroma wouldn't be this potent. Ariel preferred vanilla. He liked its scent in the cakes his mother brought. Sometimes he would ask her to come just to bring the apple pie mixed with vanilla sugar.

He stepped inside and shut the door behind him without locking it. His eyes moved steadily in every corner. His back always to the wall as he walked. He opened the doors carefully, starting with the bedroom on the right, his head moving sideways like a surveillance camera.

Ariel noticed that the curtains were drawn. Alaa only drew them when the sun crept into his bed in the morning and forced him to get up to draw them. He inherited this trait from his maternal grandmother, who left the windows open most of the time. Ariel remembered his conversation with Alaa about that and about his own maternal grandmother, Barbara, the Polish woman with striking green eyes and a pale white face. Barbara didn't like that there was so much sun in this country. She missed Poland's winters, she used to say. Ariel used to tease her by asking her why, then, did she leave Poland? She used to get angry, but later she realized that it was his way of compelling her to talk about her life there.

The burgundy comforter was crumpled over the bed. He called out "Alaa" a third time. He crossed over from the bedroom to the balcony door. There were three stools made of straw and wood surrounding a small table atop which there was an ashtray full of melon seed shells. The white damask roses and mint plant looked like tired dogs panting in the heat. Ariel picked up the empty water bottle that was next to the flowerpots and went to the kitchen through the living room. The balcony had two small doors, one leading to the bedroom, the other to the living room. He filled the bottle with water and came back to water the plants. He went back in to the living room and scrutinized everything. The coffee pot was still on the bamboo table in the middle of the room.

Alaa was an avid drinker of Arab coffee. The coffee cups were turned over their tiny saucers, which were adorned with Nile blue and dark red. Just as they had left them when they drank coffee the night before and left for Chez George's. Alaa used to look inside the cups and foretell, half seriously, what fate and the future had in store.

A *New York Times* issue fell on the Afghani carpet next to the bamboo table. Why was Ariel studying the place in such detail now? Almost like a vigilant soldier on reconnaissance.

He rummaged through his memory to remember what Alaa had told him about each item. He wanted to make sure that Alaa was still there and that he hadn't lost his mind. How can hundreds of thousands, nay millions, disappear just like that? Is it conceivable? He couldn't believe what he was thinking.

He stood in the middle of the living room, lost, looking for something out of the ordinary: a sign, or a signal. He collapsed on the coffee-colored sofa. To his right were shelves crowded with books that overflowed to the surrounding area. Bright-colored pieces of papers could be seen between the pages. Alaa was in the habit of jotting down his notes on these pieces of paper. Some of the books stacked huddled on the floor. Ariel looked away at the window to his left, as if to avoid looking at the painting Alaa had hung on the wall, right in front of him. That painting perturbed him, but his eyes returned and settled on it again, as if to devour each stroke.

Someone is lying down, or sleeping. Their body is covered with a velvet blanket. The head is covered with the Palestinian *kaffiyyah*, the way the youth wear it at protests. Nothing is visible except the eyes. Is it a male or a female? Ariel wasn't willing to stand up and go closer to read the title. The velvet blanket is adorned with bright green flowers. There is red behind, below, and inside the gray pillow. Is it blood? Is it symbolizing it?

Ariel began to feel at ease being alone in the apartment. He put his feet up on the table. Nothing was moving except his pupils, expanding and contracting as he gazed at the painting. His eyelashes batting, as if he and the veiled person were eyeing one another.

He looked away at the window again and a sense of anxiety started creeping, so he got up and went by the window. Looking at the tall trees in the median and on both sides of Rothschild Boulevard he felt that they, too, were looking back at him. He stood before the tiny table under the window. There was a red notebook on it, right next to Alaa's Apple laptop. Ariel's fingers touched the notebook as he looked at the laptop. He placed his foot on the table's pedal. It used to be a Singer sewing machine, way back before Alaa converted it to a table. Ariel doesn't usually go through his friends' stuff, but he might find a clue. He flipped open the laptop and turned it on. It asked for a password. Alaa was obsessed with Jaffa, and loved Jerusalem, where he went to work at times, too. Maybe he chose one of the two cities for his password? He typed "Jaffa" but it didn't work. Nor did "Jerusalem" in Latin letters and various spellings.

He picked up the red notebook and leafed through it. He doesn't remember seeing it before. Its last third is blank. He went back to the first page; it had Alaa's name and one sentence written in Arabic, English, and Hebrew.

If you find this notebook, that means I have lost it. Please e-mail me: alaa.assaf1967@gmail.com.
This notebook has no material value, but it does have personal value. Please return it and I'll buy you a coffee. Cheers, Alaa Assaf.

Ariel's hesitant fingers turned the pages more carefully now. He had that feeling he used to dislike back when he was doing his military service. His tasks included reading handwritten letters and translating them from Arabic to Hebrew. His father insisted that he learn Arabic because it would serve him well once he joined the army.

There was one letter he never forgot. Not because it was the first one he translated, or because the script and style of its author were so elegant, but for a reason he still cannot clearly understand. It was a letter written by a woman named Wa'd to her lover. Her lover had traveled abroad to study medicine and hadn't come back to marry her as promised. She was beseeching him to come back so they could be engaged. An engagement would have helped her withstand the pressures from her family. He kept asking her to be patient, but she sent him a farewell letter. It wasn't clear what she had meant by writing "I will not be with you when my letter reaches you." Ariel discovered later that she had committed suicide. He tried to follow what was happening to her without his superiors noticing. She, after all, was a target, and not a story that he should follow. He never knew why she committed suicide. Ariel was obsessed with her tale. His father told him to remember that he was dealing with the enemy. The plan was for him to learn Arabic in order to understand the cultural milieu and "know thy enemy" but no more.

Ariel wasn't infatuated with Arabic. He liked it, but didn't love it. His father didn't want him to be enamored with Arabic. His father was a martyr. That's what they said. The word seems strange at times, but he learned to accept it, and perhaps even feel good about it. His mother withered after that day. She kept herself busy, worked as a radio announcer, and went out with a few men, but she never regained her vitality. Something inside her was broken. After the funeral, she only listened to classical music. The funeral was without a body. He'd exploded. The chopper exploded in an instant with no prior warning. That's how Ariel imagined it because of the army's report. The circumstances of the accident were not clear, or that's what the army said. The army didn't say that things were "not clear," because the army is supposed to know everything. It said that the chopper lost communication with central command and it appears, yes "appears," that it exploded because of technical malfunction. But the army was certain that no one survived, because no one demanded a prisoner swap, despite the fact that more than one party claimed responsibility for shooting down the chopper.

He went back to Alaa's messy, even if legible, script. Looking for the last thing he'd written, he took a deep breath again, as if fearing the oxygen around him will run out. It was surprising that the last entry was from the night before, right after they had returned from Chez George's. Didn't Alaa say that he had to sleep early because he had to work the next day? Maybe he had insomnia? Ariel started reading.

16

Alaa

It is almost midnight now, and I feel so tired I cannot fall asleep. Do you remember that evening when I slept at your place in Jaffa, a month before you moved to live with my parents? I was tossing and turning in bed, and had gone to the kitchen five times to drink water. You must have heard me, because I kept shuttling between my bed, the kitchen, and the bathroom. Your voice preceded you out of the dark, and you asked me if I wanted some mint tea. As if you knew, without even asking, that I wasn't able to sleep in the room next door, and that I was staring at the silence. The silence and not the hush. "Hush" has some peace of mind, but silence is like waiting for the unknown. I smiled even before seeing your face. "That would be great." We drank the tea together without saying anything. We sat watching the silence, in and around us. That was the first time I felt you were tired of life. We sat for a whole hour and drank the whole pot of mint tea, cup after cup, exchanging a few words about the taste of mint. You said that sometimes it has a rancid taste. I disagreed, but ever since you said that, I feel it's a bit rancid. When I look back at your life, I am surprised that you didn't get tired of life until you were in your eighties. Maybe you did, but I never noticed. What am *I* tired of? Why do *I* feel so tired? You once said that a human being dies when s/he loses hope and the taste of life. Did you say all that, or am I imagining it?

"Good Night Grandson."

You said it in a night-calm voice and went to go to sleep.

"Mad, she's mad." That's what my mother said when she discovered that you'd bought and prepared your own shroud. "How did you know?" I asked her. Your grandma told me. She always referred to you using "she" and "your grandma." I rarely heard her say "my mother." You bought your shroud ten years before you departed. Ten years. Can I call your death anything but a departure? You could've stayed longer with us. Your presence brought us together and gave our lives a special flavor. You were my only grandmother. My father's folks left him with his uncle, and were forced to flee to Jordan. But they never returned. No one knows what happened to them on the road. Maybe they perished in one of the massacres? They were worried about him because he was so little. They left him with his uncle so they could put things in order in Amman first. But no one heard anything from them. They went and never came back. When we used to go on school trips to the Galilee, or any other place, I used to wonder: Should I tread lightly? Was

I walking over the corpses of those who had passed through, and who were decimated in the nakba? Was I walking over a land made of decomposed bodies? When I walk in Palestine I feel that am walking on corpses. The images of multitudes of people escaping in terror are always on my mind. All my grandparents had died, except for you. Do we inhale the decomposed corpses? What are we going to do with all this sorrow? How can we start anew? What will we do with Palestine? I, too, am tired. But whenever I wake up in the morning, I remember you and smile. And I say, just as you used to, "God will ease things." Then I listen to Fayruz singing "Yes, there is hope." Because her voice translates what you used to say, with a slight variation. I think that's what you meant by "God will ease things." But is there hope, really?

Perhaps our presence could no longer give you hope or zest? Perhaps you departed because life became bland. You said that often in your last year. Because people wither and die when they can no longer savor life. You said you didn't want to inconvenience anyone after your death, and that's why you bought the shroud. You even put the funeral expenses in a pouch, next to the shroud. But then you gave the money to charity after mother started sobbing when she knew about the whole thing. And after one of the neighbors told you it wasn't right, religiously speaking.

Your initial reaction to the neighbor was a roaring laugh. You said, "I'm not going to wait for nitwits to tell me what's right and wrong. They're smaller than my foot and have the nerves to tell me what's right." Speaking of nitwits, do you remember that afternoon when you were sitting with Um Yasmeen in your courtyard, and the proselytizing sheikhs came to lecture you about faith and religion? One of them said, with an idiotic smile, "You have to wear the veil, *Hajja*. You made the pilgrimage to Mecca and you will surely be rewarded greatly for that. But a veil and a long gown would suit your age and your faith better than this scarf, which exposes more of what it covers. Do you want to be like them Christian and Jewish women?" You shook your head and let him finish. Um Yasmeen was red in the face and was about to get up and leave. You held her hand and pushed it so she would remain seated next to you. As soon as he finished, you asked her to take off her shoe. You took it and stood up to beat him with it.

You spat on him and yelled, "Um Yasmeen's shoe is worth ten of you. Go away! You worthless imbecile. I never want to see you, or any of your kind, in this neighborhood again. I swear by the Ka'ba I visited, if I see you here again, I'll pluck your beard. Get out both of you. So, Um Yasmeen is an infidel because she's Christian? What kind of nonsense is that? Did God give you power of attorney? You have no manners and no sense, you losers."

Both of you burst out laughing. And the nitwits never dared set foot near you again. You said you saw her eyes well up. When you told me the story you said, "Where was our prophet Jesus, and his mother born anyway? Shame on these people. That's not the type of religion I learned from my folks. These idiots now claim to know God more than we do? They are God-less. There weren't any problems, not even between us and the Jews like there are today. The problems started with the Zionists. This is what my father told me. Your mother's grandpa, he was a partner with a Jewish man named Zico. And they were friends. But when the Zionists came, they kicked most people out, slaughtered them, and took everything. They ruined it and sat on top of it, as the saying goes, grandson."

I feel tired . . . always. I don't know why. Is this what you felt as the years piled on? I asked you once, when I was little, if you were scared of the soldiers, police, or of Jews, Ashkenazis in particular? You said, "No one is scary grandson. And if you are ever scared of someone, just imagine them naked, and see how most people have disgusting bodies and they look funny when they are running naked." Then you laughed heartily.

It was slightly funny, but this trick didn't appeal to me. Maybe because I was forced to undress many times. You remember the first time I went abroad, to France? They interrogated me for a long time at the airport, and they weren't satisfied with a regu-lar search. They took me to a room and left me in my underpants. I could smell the breath of the person searching me. His device made all kinds of noises as it roamed around my body. That was the first time I thought of my own skin itself as clothing. Otherwise he wouldn't have used that device on my skin, searching for something beneath. I started to sweat and you know how much I hate that. I couldn't smell my body or my own odor anymore. I was sweating like a broken water pipe.

White, white as snow, is what I felt when I was naked behind the curtain in that room. Not pure snow, but snow mixed with wet sand. There was frost coming out of the security personnel's bodies while I was sweating. We had nothing in common at that moment except our animal instincts, separated by soft gloves. Gloves touching my body as if I were nothing. A mere sheep being offered . . .

I tried to see our city, Jaffa, your city and mine, the way you saw it. I tried to walk and talk to houses and trees as if I had known them long before. As if they were your old neighbors. I would greet them and would clean the street if I saw a stray piece of paper. This is our city and these are our streets, you often said. You always picked up a piece of paper if you saw one. Do you remember when I unwrapped a piece of chocolate you bought and threw away the paper? Remember how angry you were when I, still a child back then, insisted that it was good, because it was the Jewish neighborhood? Their streets were clean and ours dirty, so why not litter their street? You said that if I loved Jaffa I must look out for it, even if it's in their hands. Their neighborhoods were still part of our city even if we weren't living in them. I didn't understand what you meant back then. But I did later.

Cities are stories and I only remember what I myself lived, or fragments from your stories and what you lived, but they are truncated. I remember *their* stories very well. The ones I learned in school, heard on TV, and read and wrote in order to pass exams. I had to tell their stories to pass in school and college. That's why I remember them like I remember my ID number. I know it by heart and can recite it any minute. I memorized their stories and their white dreams about this place so as to pass exams. But I carved my stories, yours, and those of others who are like us, inside me. We inherit memory the way we inherit the color of our eyes and skin. We inherit the sound of laughter just as we inherit the sound of tears. Your memory pains me.

They say that my laugh resembles yours, but not my mother's. Was mother's laugh like her father's? Poor mother. All that she knows about her father is that he left. After they opened the borders with Egypt, she mustered all her energy and went to Cairo to see him. He had gone there after leaving Beirut. But he died a week before she arrived. She met her half-brothers and half-sisters there, but she didn't feel they were her siblings. Some of them had the same eye color as her, but they spoke with an Egyptian accent. She was upset they didn't speak her Jaffan dialect, even though their mother was from Jaffa. Maybe she was jealous of them, because they got to grow up with a mother and a father, while she was raised fatherless. She didn't say much more about that visit. The father who was displaced from Jaffa before she was born died before she could see him. She came back sad and crestfallen. When I asked her once about her date of birth, she said she didn't like to think of it because it was the year of the nakba.

I recall some stories from your memory. The stories I read, heard, or the ones you/I made up, when you were tired. The most striking stories are the ones we make up. They are the most astounding and horrifying. What we live is truncated. Even what I lived is truncated in my memory. As if my memory is a glass house, full of cracks that are like wrinkles, but it's still standing. We can see through it, but something is muddled. "Muddled" doesn't mean a hazy view, or that both points of view are equal. These are the lies of those who write in the white books that we are forced to read. It is muddled because the pain is too great for us to endure memory. So we store it in a black box inside our heads and hearts, but it pains us and gnaws at us from within. And we rust, day after day. Yes, rust. I wonder at times why I feel all this sadness. Where does it come from? I realize soon thereafter: your memory is a burden that pains me. I feel so lonely in Jaffa.

I met Ariel today, but we didn't stay up late. Just before midnight, I told him that I had to leave because I was going to Jerusalem the next day for work. I don't know why I wanted to leave. Maybe I was bored, or wasn't interested in recalling that time when we first met. When I heard myself speaking Hebrew to Ariel,

I felt as if the voice coming out of my vocal cords was not mine. It just comes out, and speaks Hebrew on my behalf, while I am there inside myself looking and not knowing what I was doing to it, and to myself. I cannot stand this voice any longer. I felt estranged from myself. This is not the first time I have had this feeling. But it was so intense and overwhelming this time. I can't take it any longer, and am running out of patience with them. But how many times have I said this before? I say it and it doesn't matter whether I speak calmly or scream, they only see themselves. They hear, but they don't listen. Is Ariel really any different from the rest?

I hear tumult outside. I'm thinking of you a lot tonight. Tata? Are you here? I called your name, but you didn't answer. Maybe I'm at fault for not see-ing you. Perhaps I should look more carefully. I went back in and closed the balcony door. I had gone out to call you. You used to say that the best thing about city apartments and houses is their balconies. I'm lis-tening to one of your favorite songs now, Um Kul-thum's "Do You Still Remember?" I feel so cold, as if it's mid-December. White cold. White, like pure snow that will soon be sullied. White, like this white city.

I wish you were here. Missing you is like a rose of thorns.

17

Alaa

Nadeen came by yesterday to take me to Haifa to visit some friends. Nadeen, Abu Hasan's daughter, who was my classmate at the Frères school. When we finished the baccalaureate final exams, her folks decided to marry her off to her cousin. Do you remember when she came crying and begging you to convince them to postpone the marriage until after she finished college? She'd been accepted to Tel Aviv University and wanted to study there. You said that her father had gone crazy. You asked him why he'd sent her to the Frères if he didn't want her to go to college? But he was stubborn, and no one knew what got into him, and why he wanted her to get married so young.

On her wedding night, right after the party, the military intelligence came and took her husband. It looked like a prearranged deal. There were many rumors that he had made a deal with them to arrest him after the wedding. That's what people said. But it didn't make sense. Since when do the intelligence wait for someone? They placed him in security detention and she asked for a divorce, because he'd made a deal with the intelligence, and didn't even tell her he was politically active. He refused at first, but she got the divorce eventually. I'm not sure if what was said is true. I doubt it. Perhaps he was imprisoned for some civil offense, but his family claimed it was for political reasons. I don't know. The whole story doesn't hang well. I never asked her about the wedding. There were rumors about her, too. She disappeared for a period of time and we didn't know where she had gone. I loved her laugh, but she kept everyone around her at a distance. As if everyone, including her family, had betrayed her. She used to visit and we'd go out, or drink something. But she never liked to go out in Jaffa and preferred Haifa.

"What is there in Jaffa except fish restaurants and those stores in the old city the Israelis took over and turned into art studios? They fool the world trying to show American Jews and rich Russians that they've renovated and built the city. Fuck these bastards and enough already. I can't stand Jaffa any longer. I can't go out there. It hurts. And I can't stand going to these fish restaurants and hearing the owners blabber in Hebrew. I swear sometimes I can't tell who is an Arab and who is a Jew. For the love of God, let's get away from Jaffa. Haifa is much better."

"You're overdoing it," I used to tell her. But I had no objection to going to Haifa. There is no city like it. Coming from a Jaffan, that's high praise. The sea has a different face there. Would you have objected had you heard me say this about Haifa? Anyway,

where was I? Yes, I was visiting my folks and I went
to the flea market. I was looking for an old chair to go
along with the 1970s green set in the guest room. It's
still in our house. My mother didn't want to throw
it away. It wasn't really used since we, as you know,
never sat in the guest room that often. I was looking
for a chair from that period. I thought I'd send it to be
refurbished along with the whole set. When I passed
by stores in the flea market I would see very old furniture, from the 1940s. I used to wonder whether it
was old and refurbished, or looted from the houses of
those who were forced to flee? I sometimes have an
intense feeling of anger and bitterness when I walk in
Jaffa. I feel am on the cusp of madness. And I wonder
how you were able to stay in Jaffa without going mad
yourself.

I stood before a big oval mirror with wood lin-
ing topped by an engraving in the shape of a bunch
of grapes. The storeowner had probably repainted it
recently. I remembered you as I looked at myself in
the mirror. The beauty mark on my right cheek is the
same as the one you had. My mother had it, too, but
on her left cheek. I looked at my hoary curly hair. My
eyes look tired and have black circles around them. Is
it true that my eyes have the same color as my grandfather's? Why didn't you say that they were blue like
my mother's? Why were you so cruel to her? As if
depriving her of the pleasure of having me look like
her. Why did you always remind her of the man who
left when she was still in your womb?

I remembered the story about the mirror and curtains.

You told me that what pained you the most were the mirror and the curtains you left behind in your house. You didn't retrieve them when you went back, even though you stayed in Jaffa? They kicked you out of al-Manshiyye, but you stayed in Jaffa. They took you from your homes and crammed you in other houses in Ajami and surrounded you with barbed wire. I remembered your story about the mirror. You were too shy when you were married. He took your hand and you both stood before the mirror. He told you, "Look into the mirror and see how gorgeous you are. Don't be shy." Then he started to touch you and caress your body right there in front of the mirror. That's what you said, and it stayed with me. Mother went crazy when she heard you talk about sex so explicitly in my presence. Maybe she was angered by something else too. That you were talking about the father she never got to know. How sweet and loving he was, but not to her. She got upset whenever you cracked one of your lewd jokes. You and I laughed a lot and you told her that she was too uptight. "Jaffans like to joke around and to live life," you'd say. You were baffled that she was like that. "She's so backward. I swear. She harps on shame and manners so often, one would think she's the mother and am her daughter." Then you sighed and didn't say much afterward. You felt tired and asked me to go with you to your house, which was a fifteen-minute walk away.

That was before you moved to live with us the last six months.

"Iskandar Awad," I used to repeat whenever I went through Razyal Street, the name that had occupied Iskandar Awad Street. After they uprooted the street's name, they gave it a number. They replaced street names with numbers. They kept the names that had remained naked, then they dressed them up in foreign names. I try to remind myself out loud of the names of streets, houses, and people who live here . . . still live here. Even if they are now in Beirut, Amman, or any other place. I know their tales and problems. I know who got married and who didn't. How you all spent your holidays, the orchards, and Prophet Rubin festivities. I never understood who this Rubin was, and why you stopped celebrating his feast? "So what if Israel came? Why would you stop celebrating him?" I asked you once when I was young. God. I realize now how cruel our questions can be sometimes.

I was cruel when I was young. I didn't get much of what you used to say. I never appreciated the Jaffa you spoke of. I thought you were exaggerating. Otherwise why did they leave? I know they were kicked out, but sometimes it seems that words cannot convey the cruelty of what took place. I didn't understand. Only later did I comprehend what it meant when you said, "Bullets were flying over our heads, darling. To stay was like committing suicide. It was terrifying and it all happened in a flash. God have mercy on our loved ones, the dead and the living. That's enough darling. My heart aches."

I told you once that, with you, I felt that I was living the world of your Jaffa before "that year." I live in an entire world above, or beneath (it doesn't matter) the city we live in. You didn't like me saying that Jaffa was buried beneath Jaffa. You said that Jaffa will always be Jaffa. It exists everywhere around us. We just have to look to see. You said that you could hear voices and wedding celebrations with music and drums at night. Mother said you were crazy. "Only you, and those who don't hear the drums at night, are crazy," you said to anyone who doubted your words. You drove me crazy talking about al-Manshiyye and even Tel Aviv. You said you used to go to Allenby Street to buy cloth for brides. You were a seamstress and that is what saved you from the claws of poverty.

You said you cried a lot when you went back and rang the bell of your house in al-Manshiyye after they'd forced you to leave it and go to Ajami. One day you snuck away with your father to retrieve the guest room curtains. You never explained how you managed to sneak away. "We went," you said. I never asked how you were able to do that when you were still under military rule. You told your father that you'd crocheted those curtains with your blind sister, Sumayya, and hung them before she, your mother, brother, and Ruben left Palestine. They all tried to save their lives and were hoping that your father could convince you to leave and you would return later. He didn't want to leave you by yourself, especially since your husband had been displaced to Beirut.

There was a woman living there, in your own home, and she recognized you. She knew that you were the owner without you saying a single word. You sat in your house and she offered you coffee. You were embarrassed to ask for the curtains. She said the curtains were beautiful and she'd never seen crocheted curtains before. You didn't comment. You left with your father and felt that you had betrayed Sumayya. Your father didn't say anything either. He remained silent as if tongue-tied. And he died soon thereafter. He went mad and then died. He was demented and then died. How can I describe his condition? You described it differently each time. He left you and mother alone. He was demented, as if he couldn't bear staying in Jaffa without becoming demented. I still imagine you walking together, greeting strangers in your city, and smiling so that he would be reassured that all was well. Why am I telling you, again, what you already told me? Perhaps I am writing out of fear, and against forgetfulness. I write to remember, and to remind, so as memories are not erased. Memory is my last lifeline.

What am I saying to you? How can I describe what I feel? I feel intense loneliness. I'm orphaned without you. My mother was never more than a caring woman, but I forgot that she was my mother. My father was way too busy with work. Sometimes I am so sad I cannot cry. Is that what you meant when you said, "Tears have dried up in Jaffa"? I wish you had stayed longer and never left us.

Where are we? Oh, yes, I was telling you about Nadeen, our neighbor, and how I survived death. I was standing before that mirror at the flea market in Jaffa, imagining that intimate moment with you and the grandfather I never knew. Memories, mine and yours, flash suddenly. I was smiling, as if I had seen you in the mirror, when I heard a voice calling my name. It was Nadeen. You liked her joie de vivre and sense of humor. We hugged. She had a slender body and smelled good always. She told me that she'd finished college, and was working as a teacher in al-Lid, but she didn't want to stay there, because the situation was horrible.

"Things are so tough here in Jaffa, I never thought there could be worse. But it's much worse over there. I just can't go on. Students boast that their fathers are drug dealers. One of them even brought a gun to school, and the principal didn't do anything. Can you believe that? They are drowning in drugs and a form of tribalism that has nothing to do with old Bedouin values, or their city life. It's a hodgepodge and the state leaves it as is so that they keep wallowing in drugs, crime, and being lost. They don't need to do anything, or bother with these youth, because they're already lost. It's hopeless."

"But Nadeen, if everyone leaves, who will change things? Their situation is not worse than blacks, or

Native Americans, in the US. Nevertheless, they try
to change things."

"Alaa, darling, spare me your naiveté. Native
Americans are almost gone and the blacks are still suffering. You know what? You are right. We shouldn't
leave, but I can't anymore. If you want, you can leave
Tel Aviv and go to al-Lid to work with these kids.
But, please don't pontificate, because I'm really tired
of slogans."

I didn't want to defend myself or what I do, so I
told her that it was a complicated subject and we'll
agree to disagree. She insisted on coming by the next
day to take me to Haifa, so I told her we'd resume our
argument then.

I spent most of last week at my parents' house.
Mother is not doing so well. She's sick. The doctor
says she's depressed. She says that she's just sick and
the doctor is an idiot. I felt that she needed me to be
by her side. But let me tell you how we escaped death
yesterday.

Nadeen came in her old Volkswagen Golf. My
mother frowned upon my going out with her. She
thought that she had designs on me, especially since
she was a divorcée. I tried to explain to my mother
that I saw her by accident and neither of us was interested in a relationship. We were like siblings. But
mother didn't get it.

I am going on and on. When I write in this red
notebook I feel that you are here, sitting and listening

to me. It is still difficult for me to call your departure "death." This word carries the sense of eternal loss. Anyway, we left Jaffa and were heading to Haifa. We didn't take the express highway, because Nadeen wanted to stop by Tel Aviv University to drop off books to a friend of hers there. It's never a straightforward trip with her. We always end up making unplanned stops to buy something, or see someone. We sat at the cafeteria to have a coffee about an hour after we'd left Jaffa. Mother called, but I didn't answer. She kept calling. I got worried so I answered. Her voice was shaky. She said that a suicide bomber had detonated his car at the Beit Lid intersection. Had we gone directly to Haifa we would've been at the intersection around the time of the bombing. Were it not for Nadeen's random decisions, our lives, or deaths, would have intersected with that man's. They said on the news that he was a father of five from the Galilee.

It seems that I have dodged death more than once. Do you remember the year I had to live part of the time in Jerusalem for work? There were many suicide operations. Cell phones were not widely used back then. I didn't have one. But I would know that I had escaped death when the landline kept ringing in the early morning. I would hear my mother's terrified voice when I picked up. She used to call to make sure I was still asleep. I always missed the early morning bus and death would miss me. I hated working as a cameraman those days. Having to hear the chants of "*Mavat la'Aravim!*" (Death to Arabs!). The jarring sound of that chant still resounds in my head. Sometimes I would be looking into the mirror and I would sarcastically repeat these chants. As if trying to drive away the fear that nests in my memory.

I was never that close to death. Maybe when we are born in such a place, on a cradle of disasters, we always search for riveting stories about surviving life and death. Because "normal" stories don't resemble us. We no longer see ourselves in our stories—the ones in which we tend to our boredom. So we search for ourselves elsewhere, so we may resemble our images in news stories and novels. Why did I just switch to writing in the plural? Everything around me is fragmented.

Tata, I miss you . . . a lot!

Ariel turned the page and felt uncomfortable that Alaa was not honest with him the previous night. He didn't say that he was tired or bored. Why did he lie and say that he had to go to work today? It was the last page. Ariel looked at his watch and realized he had to go back to his apartment and write his article.

He understood now why Alaa always talked about his grandmother and rarely mentioned his mother. But why did he lie? Their conversation the night before was normal. They didn't talk about politics. Was it just Alaa's need for solitude? Ariel felt a lump in his throat. He closed the red notebook and kept it in his lap. He turned on the lamp to his right.

The veiled person's eyes in the painting on the wall across from him glistened as they gazed at him. It was strange, he thought, that a painting could unsettle him. He grabbed the red notebook and got up to go to his apartment.

He left the light on.

18

Ariel

He felt sluggish climbing the ten steps separating the two apartments. A breeze from the balcony door he'd left open caressed his face as soon as he entered. He went to the kitchen to make coffee.

He sat before the small brown round Italian table. He lifted the white cup, bringing it close to his nose to draw in the coffee's aroma. He opened a new document on his laptop and typed his name, the city, and the date.

The cursor kept blinking. He moved the chair closer to the table and tried to sit properly. The doctor had advised him to do that after suffering severe back pain. He pulled the drawer and took out the special towelette to clean the screen. He will postpone listening to music until later. He needs to focus now. He took a deep breath. The cursor is still blinking.

It's best to start with the title. That makes it easier. He typed "Where did they go?" but he deleted it right away. It's not appropriate for a newspaper article, not the one he wrote for. The editors liked his column. It had a sizable readership and generated debate at times. The newspaper he wrote for was midrange. It had only three offices outside the US: in Tel Aviv, Brussels, and Hong Kong. But it was well known, and he was its sole correspondent in the country. His office was tiny and dim, so he preferred to work at his apartment sometimes.

He left the title, the blank page, and the chair to light his first cigarette of the day. He doesn't smoke a lot; three cigarettes per day, if any. He went out to the balcony and stood there watching pedestrians and buses. The latter seemed to have calibrated arrival and departure times better than earlier that day.

He saw a woman pacing back and forth inside the bus stop. She appeared tense and kept looking at her watch. The glass had been broken for more than a month now, but the municipality had yet to fix it. One of the four plastic seats was broken as well. He felt as if the atmosphere around her was growing tense as well. Why does she keep looking at her watch? It will not hasten the arrival of the bus. He, too, looked at his watch. It was two thirty in the afternoon.

Waiting. Yes! That's the best way to begin his column. Now he has a beginning. He finished his cigarette in a hurry and went back inside.

19

Ariel

Tel Aviv—Ariel Levy

Waiting reigns in Tel Aviv as it faces the most dangerous challenge since independence. The city's streets are full of waiting and anticipation. The question on everyone's mind is: What is happening? And perhaps the other most important question is: Who knows what is happening?

The government spokesman, Yair Kanun, has held two press conferences so far. The first was at eleven this morning, followed by a second one two hours later. There was nothing new in either. He didn't add to what the media had reported since the morning. It seems that the objective of the press conferences was psychological rather than to provide any information about what is taking place. As if Kanun wanted to reassure Israelis, and the rest of the world, that we are still fine and alive, and that the Israeli government and security forces are in control. The second press conference was attended by Yigal Goldman, the official spokesperson of the IDF. Both men stressed several points.

The first was an internal message of reassurance for Israelis. The second was a message to our allies abroad to say that all is under control. The third was to enemy states that are watching. The overarching message was that "our people are fine."

It reminds me of the song that was broadcast on state TV in 1991, after Saddam Hussein fired Scud missiles on Tel Aviv and its environs. After the news, they played Ofra Haza's "Alive."

The song had reached second place in the Eurovision contest in Germany in 1983.

But beyond songs, tactics, and soon-to-be-forgotten press statements, what do we actually know so far? There is no trace of Palestinians in the country. This sentence has been repeated like a broken record since this morning. Is this conceivable? Can we believe that the Palestinians disappeared? Without a drop of blood? What about Palestinians in the diaspora and in the camps? The news indicates that they are still there, but does this mean they will start crawling toward us?

Is the government and the IDF responsible for their disappearance? If the army is involved, can we imagine that such a bold step would have been taken without the knowledge of the American administration? I don't think this speculation holds any water. I don't think the Palestinians have been annihilated. These are accusations leveled by some organizations, Arab governments, and Palestinian factions abroad. The goal seems to be to calm their constituencies.

Moreover, pointing fingers at Israelis and holding them responsible for whatever ill befalls Palestinians is something to which Israelis are accustomed. This doesn't mean that the government or security forces were not aware of what was being planned. But it is highly unlikely that they were involved in planning it. We are at the outset of our search and one might find a trace. Accusations and questions fly and there are yet to be any clear answers.

Perhaps the Palestinians have disappeared, and that's all there is to it. A listener called a radio station this morning to express his anger at the attention this event is getting. He called on everyone to go out to the street to celebrate "that this problem disappeared on its own. It is a divine miracle." Only a few crazed extremists responded to his call. The rest of the Israelis are in a state of anticipation.

At any rate, the great majority of Israelis are not that interested in the daily lives of Palestinians. Israelis want peace of mind, but they also want security, and that is their chief concern. This is quite understandable if we consider the racism, persecution, and killing this people have suffered, and the wars this relatively young nation has had to fight. All this doesn't mean that the majority will be satisfied if the IDF, or state institutions, committed an unethical act against the Palestinians.

Another theory holds the other side, i.e., Palestinians, or perhaps Arabs, responsible for the disappearance. It assumes that the Palestinians have started a general strike. But the problem in this theory is that the strike was not announced beforehand, as is customary. Moreover, there are usually protests and statements declaring the strike's demands. None of this happened. More importantly, in taking part in a strike, even if not going to work or going outside to public places, one still has to *be* somewhere. And Palestinians are neither at home, nor anywhere else. The police and IDF have raided houses in many neighborhoods and have not found a single Palestinian in the country as of now.

The search continues in full swing in the Galilee forests, Jerusalem, and Judea and Samaria. In addition to the reconnaissance missions of the air force, police and army units are conducting a comprehensive sweep of every inch in Israel. So the various scenarios about the disappearance of the Palestinians have yet to offer a fruitful, or even logical, answer.

A source in the army (who spoke on condition of anonymity) said, "It wouldn't be an exaggeration to say that the forty-eight hours following the first mass disappearance of Arabs will determine the direction the state will take and its steps in the future."

So, let us wait out the remaining thirty hours to see what they may bring. Waiting is hellish, but it is the only option.

k

Ariel read his article twice. He revised some sentences and changed the word order here and there. Then he logged into his e-mail and wrote a short message to Matthew:

Dear Matthew,
    Here is the article. I'll send another one as soon as I have any new information. I will try to interview some representatives from the army and government. I'm still waiting for confirmation from their press offices. Will let you know later. Let me know if you have any comments on the piece.
                    More soon
                    Ariel

He turned up the volume on his radio so as not to miss any breaking news. He made sure that his ringer and breaking news notifications on his cell were both loud enough. He felt the urge to read Alaa's notebook.

20

Alaa

Has my heart become numb? What does it mean that someone's heart becomes numb? How? Does it become numb when one stops posing questions? Maybe my heart has withered? Have their hearts withered? How could we walk the same path, and look at the same sea, yet see something completely different?

I look at my old photographs to see the person I was twenty years ago. I recognize myself and see that my photographs resemble me. But I don't see myself. The older I get, the more I look more like my father. He has aged a lot this past year. I must tell you something important. He is going to stop working as a surgeon. How shall I say it? He is still working, but his illness exhausts him. His eyesight is very weak and there is no remedy. The doctor told him that he will be completely blind in two to three years. He's changed a lot. You know how he doesn't like to rely on anyone. He stays silent a lot. Yes, it's not that he speaks so little. He stays silent. He resembles a cactus. A cactus with no fruit, just full of thorns.

I don't know him well. I told you once that I grew up like an orphan. You were very upset when I said that. But my father was always busy with work. Do you know that most of my memories with him are beautiful, because I didn't know him that well? He was rarely at home. Shuttling from one surgery to the next. I thought he was a butcher. How else could I explain his obsession with surgeries? My mother, on the other hand, was busy with everything in the house and around it: people, neighbors, and even dust.

Yesterday marked twenty days since they bombed Gaza. That's what I initially wanted to say, but didn't want to start with it. They were pulling corpses out of the rubble as if they were dolls. They pull, but the corpses refuse to come out of the debris. They were covered with dust and blood. I had a strong urge to go and wipe the dust off myself. Maybe because I wanted to see the faces clearly. I say "bombed Gaza" and not "declared war on it," because "war" sounds lighter. "War" was a big word when I was young. But I grew bigger and it grew smaller. There are so many wars around us we've gotten used to them. I never experienced bombing and that's why it always seemed severe and hard. There is an absurd repetition in bombing. When we were kids we used to play "War Started in . . ." We used to draw a circle and divide it according to the number of players. We gave each part the name of a country. We would often choose names like Lebanon, Palestine, Iraq, and Egypt. No one ever chose Saudi Arabia or Morocco.

One of us would then hold a branch and say, "The war started in . . . Lebanon," and then throw the branch away from the person who chose the name of that country, and that person would have to catch the others. I hated that game. Not because it involved war, but because I never liked running after someone and catching them. Did you use to play it too? I don't remember that someone taught me how to play it, or any other game. As if these games grew up with me. What types of games did you play when you were a kid? I don't remember you telling us much about your childhood. Except a few sentences in passing. How come I never realized that before? Weren't you a child once? You were a youth, a young woman, a wife, a mother, a grandmother, and a seamstress. But you were never a child.

Forget about games and childhood, and let's go back to bombing. As I mentioned, they bombed Gaza. They bombed them with airplanes and bombs, and what else? My heart is numb. Maybe my heart has withered and the hearts of those they bombed have become numb. I looked for you yesterday. I went out to the streets, the sea, and to that spot where I found you. I stood there for a while, hoping that something would pass by indicating that there is life after death. But you weren't there. How can I say what I want to say to you? Father. He is gone as well. Yes. He left three days ago. My mother called me in the morning crying. "You have to come. Your father is very sick."

I took a taxi and went home. Dr. Abed, the one you called a chatterbox, was there. Baba is gone, Tata. He died before I got to know him well.

The truth is he committed suicide. But we didn't tell anyone, because suicide is shameful. We didn't tell anyone. His death seemed normal after all these days of bombing Gaza.

I looked for you and didn't find you. I wanted to tell you that they bombed Gaza and that Baba committed suicide.

I went toward the al-Bahr Mosque and couldn't find you. I didn't find you.

Baba committed suicide and they bombed Gaza for the twentieth day.

Baba's suicide was trivial after all these days of them bombing Gaza.

21

Alaa

The houses on Rothschild Street, where I live, line up like a column of soldiers. Since I was born, Tel Aviv's houses have been washed up in the city's whiteness, or vice versa. There are things that are born all at once. A building is memory. Cities and places without old buildings have no memory. Maybe I say this because I am from an old city. Bedouins will see memory in other places. What matters is that I am the son of an ill-fated city. Jaffa is my ill-fated city. But what about cities that are born all at once? Are there such cities?

Tel Aviv is full of Bauhaus architecture. Its memory is buildings and houses washed in whiteness. Memory is a choice. Memory is gray. That's what Ariel says when we discuss this subject. Lies, I say. There is no gray memory. There are flashes that come in one burst and are as clear as a sword's blade. Either black or white. There is no gray in between. But white and black come in shades. Gray is what is confusing, and we confuse what we want to confuse. Didn't I say, time and again, that there is a fissure in my memory? Your memory, which inhabits mine, has a fissure. The fissure doesn't mean obscurity. The fissure is pain.

Why do I always imagine Baron Rothschild cutting the ribbon at the street's official inauguration? I don't even remember seeing such a photograph. But he was here on some spot in this street. When I walk the city's streets, I touch its houses with my looks. I hear myself screaming out loud. As if a clear glass separates me from the people around me. Glass that shields sounds. I rarely see it, but I know that it is there when I scream and no one hears me.

I sit in the middle of the boulevard. Yes, Rothschild is a boulevard and not a street. I don't know why I call it "street." I sit on the wooden benches that sit, together with trees, in the middle of the street. Waiting and I sit together. I don't know what I am waiting for, but I am waiting for something. Sometimes I even dream that I'm sitting and waiting. I dream that I'm waiting. What a silly dream!

When evening creeps in, the lights of houses and cafes around me appear, and I wait. That's not a dream. That is what I actually do as I sit on the benches that are surrounded with giant trees in the median. As if the buildings around me, from which lights and shadows appear, are also waiting for someone, or something. Everything is beautiful from the vantage point of the bench. As soon as night falls, I begin to wash the houses around me with black memory. I wipe the whiteness off the facades of buildings and paint everything black. I take black from the night's kohl and draw the city black. As if I am afraid that the white memory will possess me, so I wipe it with the blackness of a moonless night. I love the color black because it resembles us. It is us.

Sometimes I leap out of the bench like a clock spring and walk in stammering steps to the sea. I see nothing around me, because I've colored all the houses with black. Even the moon is black. I often go through Shenkin Street. I greet the people sitting at coffee shops. They smile and call out, "Alaa! Come sit with us! Let's chat and have a glass of wine . . . tell us about Jaffa and your Jaffan grandmother. Come on!" I imagine them being genuinely interested and asking what never crosses their mind . . . How do *we* feel? How do *we* live? But questions no longer have any meaning. I leave them without responding. I no longer care to tell them anything. Everyone welcomes me. They all want to hear my stories and yours. Yes, your stories! My stories are fissures of your stories. The ones you told me, and the ones you never did. What a big lie. I pay them no attention and go on. I leave Shenkin Street and pass through the small streets of al-Karmil Market until I reach the sea. This is not a dream. I do this time and again. I imagine and hear people saying what they say. I imagine that I paint everything around me black and see no other color. Black is beautiful.

I reach the sea to catch a glimpse of your city as it shimmers at night. But its lights are faint. Like a corpse cast on the seashore. You will say that Jaffa hasn't died. I didn't say it has. "Corpse" is used to describe a pulsating body in Arabic. Don't we say, "He has a huge corpse"? The youth in Ajami say, "Man, his corpse is like that of a mule."

Here, on Jaffa's shores, the sea looks exhausted. Jaffa doesn't scream the way I do. It stammers. But those who inhabit it don't hear what it says. There is something in this corpse, Jaffa, that no one in the White City understands. Is this what you felt when you said that the city's mornings were tired and had left "that year"? You didn't say it exactly like that. But you said, "Our morning was like a widowed man. His beloved died and love disappeared."

What if we were to scream into their ears? Would they hear us? We could pull their ears and scream. Would they hear us? I had a strange dream yesterday. You'd laugh if I told you about it. I dreamt of a huge square. I keep walking to its end but it kept moving farther. It was full of people—crowds like ants. I don't know why I thought they were Palestinians. What does it mean to be Palestinian? Anyway, someone, speaking very calmly, unlike orators do in squares before crowds, decided that the only solution was that we convert to Judaism. No one objected. Everyone agreed and we solved the question of Palestine. When I woke up in the morning I went online to see if this was true. You would've laughed at my dream and told me, "It wouldn't make any difference, dear."

Do you know that when father committed suicide, mother found him in his bed? He took poison.

I don't know which kind. Mother refused to give me a copy of the hospital report or talk about the details. I don't know if he suffered. Mother took care of everything. It looks like she'll only rest when she is dead. She turns one page after another, and with each, she turns over one of the lives of those around her: her father, who remained a blank page, you, and then her husband. She doesn't see me. I don't know why I imagine my mother's corpse is the city's corpse. Her hysterectomy and sickness, and father being too busy for her, crushed her heart. She didn't die. She's still alive. Corpses are our living bodies. But she's the nakba generation. Those who were born when the nakba was born. They know how to give, but don't know how to express affection. What can I tell you? I think you were cruel to her, but . . .

22

Alaa

I sit on the coffee-brown sofa in the living room of my apartment on Rothschild Boulevard. The one you slept on once when you visited me. You were tired because we had walked so much that day. Do you remember how you said, "Oh, sweetheart. Why do you have a painting of a man with his face covered hanging on your wall? Why not roses, or Jaffa . . . or maybe a pretty girl . . . and why is everything in the background red as if he's bleeding . . . poor boy . . . Why do you hang such depressing paintings? Put one of a beautiful woman, not a man whose face is covered and is surrounded with blood." I laughed a lot and didn't say anything. I don't know why this painting bothers a lot of people. When I came back to the room after making coffee for both of us, you'd fallen asleep. I went out and drank the whole pot by myself on the balcony.

My handwriting is annoying today because am lying down on the sofa as I write. Maybe it's better to sit at the sewing machine I converted into a table. I love it and know very well that it carried your pain and loneliness and still remembers them. You used to tell me, "You couldn't imagine how lonely we felt in our country that year when everyone left and we stayed . . . we were like orphans. We were orphaned. The most difficult thing is to be orphaned in one's own home, and then people from abroad arrive and become the home owners . . . Enough, sweetheart, enough!"

Maybe we are still like that. Maybe we are still orphans.

I took your sewing machine from mother and converted it to a small table. The sewing machine you worked on for decades making wedding gowns. The machine that exhausted your feet and wore them down, but saved you and allowed mother to enter the Teachers' College and get married. Do you remember it? You must, since you used to boast about it all the time. You were afraid that mother would throw it away. "Your mother is crazy and only leaves rags around her, but throws away all good things." As I mentioned once before, mother took out all your clothes after you left and gave them to the poor. She didn't keep a single piece. She should have. I was angry and fought with her and made her cry. She said they had your scent, and whenever she passed by them she smelled it and thought you'd enter the house any minute. She used to sit and cry for you. The house is empty. Mother is afraid that they would demolish it if they knew that no one was living in it. She said that I should go back and live there. But it's a tiny house and I don't think they would grant us the permit to repair it. It's so chilly there, but, I'm thinking seriously about going back. Mother goes there every day. Makes her coffee, sits in the small courtyard, smokes her cigarette, and waters the flowers. She misses you, but never says it and just cries in silence, as if summoning you. I've never seen anyone cry the way she does. As if the tears flow from her skin pores and not her eyes.

She kept all your photographs, even hung some of them on the living room wall. I was surprised, because she never used to look at or talk about them when you were still alive. Do you remember the one in which she's wearing her engagement dress? It was glittery, the color of almond blossoms. You sewed it yourself, just as you sewed all her dresses. It was taken in 1966, a year before I was born. How old was she back then? Eighteen? It shows her standing there with a timid smile. Father on her right, and you on her left. My father's uncle and his wife next to you. My father was an orphan. Maybe his parents were alive, but I doubt it. Otherwise why didn't they come back to take him? Why did they leave him with his uncle and never inquire about him? Maybe they died on the road when they had to flee? He lived with his uncle whom he loved a lot. But he didn't love his wife. His relationship with his cousins was complicated. After his uncle's death, he only saw them at feasts and on major occasions. How did he get to study medicine? Was his family wealthy? If so, where is the money? He's been a doctor ever since I can remember. He travelled abroad a lot to conferences. Did he have affairs there? I don't know. His trips abroad used to annoy my mother, but she lost interest later. Or her interest faded and became that of a typical spouse, especially after she had that major surgery. I didn't know anything at first, but later on I discovered that it was a hysterectomy. We were doing well, financially, but not that great. Our house didn't look like a surgeon's house. It was big and beautiful, but hadn't been renovated in the last twenty-five years. Mother used to complain that my father worked half of the time for free, and that he should've taken fees to help his family instead of spending it on strangers.

I don't know my father's relatives who stayed in Jaffa that well. I see them during visits and at weddings, but that's it. You said once that he rarely talks to them "because they exploited him and short-changed him with the inheritance." I never understood why you never spoke about these matters unambiguously. "Shush" was the answer to any questions about these subjects. I never liked to attend weddings. They were quite boring and miserable. You used to say that most of my father's relatives, like your relatives, were scattered all over the world. Some in Kuwait, others in Jordan, Iraq, Lebanon, and the rest somewhere else.

I realized today that you were heavy. Your bare shoulders and arms look huge in the photograph. Don't get upset. I'm just teasing. You were always beautiful. Who said that being thin is beautiful any-way? I know you'll say that I'm a liar and that all my girlfriends were as thin as broomsticks. Maybe I do prefer thin women, but I don't necessarily think they are more attractive than heavy ones. Do you remember how you sat among your many visitors boasting about Jaffa? You used to utter words I didn't understand, like "Prophet Rubin." Which prophet was he? And why did you ask me to name my son after him if I get married and have a child? Rubin, the name of your brother and the prophet you used to celebrate.

The Jaffa I grew up in was full of fear, poverty, ignorance, and racism. Full of those who look like us, walk on two feet, but, for a reason I didn't understand at the time, scorn us. That's what it seemed like to me at the time. No, it didn't "seem." I heard it with my own ears. I heard them cursing me, so I cursed them back. I used to be afraid of them when I was a child. Now I've learned not to see only them. I see them and see my own shadow whenever I see them. Sometimes I see myself walking next to them and sitting in their homes. It's strange for me to say that their homes are their homes. Sometime I don't wish to see them. Just like that, and for no reason.

I love Jaffa just as you loved it, but in my own way. Maybe we love it equally. I don't know, and it's not important. I won't deny that I hate it sometimes. Tourists come to our neighborhoods just to watch. And others offer exorbitant prices to buy our houses.

They used to come and watch us, as if we were monkeys in a zoo.

My feet used to take me to walk northward, to that other city whose name they stuck onto Jaffa's name. I pass by the old city houses overlooking the sea. The ones the artists and the affluent have usurped. They're like a museum. Who observes whom in these museums? The exhibits or the visitors? Do they feel, even for a moment, that these houses are stolen? Are they haunted? I want to believe that the spirits of those who used to live in them are still there, seeking comfort. Maybe what actually happens is that it all comes to an end and nothing more. Had there been a God, this would not have happened. I've thought a great deal about this and I even told you once. Do you remember? You became angry and didn't speak to me for a week. You didn't forgive me until I fasted a whole day for you. And you know that I am not friends with fasting. That was the only time I fasted my entire life. I did it just for you. You said you were sad when "they stuck Tel Aviv's name to Jaffa. Just like someone being up your ass. You don't see them and they never let go." The image cracked me up. Mother protested, "Shame on you for saying such things at your age." You laughed and didn't respond.

I used to ask you often why your relatives left, but you stayed? You'd remain silent for a couple of minutes and then say, "There is no answer, dear. It was a coincidence that we stayed. They left because they had to leave. Do you know what kind of bombing we endured? There were explosions every day. They killed people and threw them out on the street. Do you know how many buildings collapsed on our heads? No one leaves their country just like that. Leaving was like suicide, and staying was suicide too." Then you'd fall silent as if you departed and went back to those moments. I was trying to understand. I asked you even more frequently as I grew older. You grew more silent.

How can anyone who knew Jaffa leave it? I say it and am embarrassed. I say it realizing that the narrative of the White City's people about the brunette city has seeped into my memory. It's the lie of whiteness. Their memory has seeped into mine. How can I sweep it out of mine? Is it possible? Even if I do, there will still be a trace. Is this the toll we have to pay for staying here?

You were a woman who spoke for herself and never let anyone speak for you. You even spoke for others sometimes. Is that why mother spoke so little? Speech was almost a defective act for her. You were the mistress of words. I used to love chatting with you so much. Perhaps the angrier women are, the more silent they become. Is mother often silent because she's the angriest among us?

*

Ariel's phone rang. He flipped the edge of the page he was reading. It was his mother. He didn't listen well at first because he was still occupied with what he'd just read. He was confused a bit, so he took a deep breath, as if drawing a line to separate his thoughts from his mother's voice on the phone. She was asking too many unanswerable questions, punctuated with "but you are a journalist." He was about to tell her that he wasn't a news agency, and even news agencies with their network of correspondents and journalists don't have a clue as to what's happening. But he sensed fear conquering him, too, and only said what would set her mind at ease.

23

Ariel

He called some friends and acquaintances to see if it was possible to go into any of the Arab areas in the country, or to Arab houses in Jaffa. There were Jews living in many of these neighborhoods, and one could go there. He was told that all these houses and neighborhoods were surrounded with police and army units. They didn't allow anyone to enter without a search and a check on IDs and addresses to make sure they lived there. He had to wait.

Is the army clearing the area there, or did the Palestinians really disappear? Our army can never do such a thing. Have they made mistakes? Yes, but at the end of the day they follow laws and adhere to humanist values. Who doesn't make mistakes? They do everything according to international norms. Sometimes they're not fair, true. But is there absolute justice in this world? Where was it during the Holocaust? Our founding fathers were wise. They predicted that these catastrophes would take place. And that's why they came here. Ariel sighed deeply, as if trying to hold on to this thought, and to prevent other ones from taking its place. What is most important now is for him to figure out what is happening.

He moved to the bedroom and turned the TV on before lying in bed. He felt the evening grip him by the neck and was anxious about the coming hours. He took a deep breath and exhaled very slowly. He stared at the ceiling and found himself wondering how the country would be, were there no Palestinians in it. He wished he could drive out all these thoughts and just stare at the light reflection on the ceiling. To think of nothing except colors. He thought of rolling a joint, but he needs a clear head. He has to stay alert these days. He spent half an hour staring at the ceiling and listening to the TV. Then he got out of bed, turned the TV off, and went to the living room. He put his laptop and Alaa's notebook in his black bag. He added the key to Alaa's apartment to his keychain and headed to Chez George.

24

Rothschild Boulevard

Ariel walked nimbly. Rothschild Boulevard was still there with its trees and tiny white buildings. Tel Aviv seemed tame and tranquil, as if it had renounced its reputation as a restless city. That evening, for the first time in its tiny history, since the first brick was laid in the first settlement, the city stopped, to take a deep breath and contemplate what was taking place around it. Tel Aviv is small and beautiful with its big, clean, and dreamy beaches. It's a dream come true! A dream that started with a tiny step but came true. It doesn't matter how, or at what price. What matters is that it came true. Ariel paused before each of these passing thoughts. Had he been writing them down he would've underlined or bolded some of them.

The streets were almost empty. Most people were nailed in front of their TV screens, whose lights were reflected on the walls and curtains of the buildings he passed by. The sounds were escaping through the windows. He looked at the chinaberries, cypresses, palm trees, and the younger sycamores, which were planted way back in the 1930s. He tripped on a pebble, or a bump, because the street wasn't paved properly.

He crossed to the other side and passed between two sycamores. He stood to gaze at no. 16. It was here, in Dizengoff House, that Ben Gurion read the Declaration of Independence, at 4 p.m. on the 14th of May, 1948. Eight hours before the end of the British Mandate. Wasn't that a miracle? That we returned after 3,000 years? His excitement was about to move his lips to say it out loud.

He remembered when Alaa said once that he hated the street and this building. Ariel asked him, "Why do you live on a street you hate?" "Because this is *my* Palestine, and I want to live wherever I please, even streets that whip me. I don't want to stay in our ghettos, because I'm not a stranger here." Ariel thought Alaa's answer was odd at the time, and felt that he was addressing Ariel and implying that *he* was the stranger.

What did Alaa want? Were we to recognize what Alaa sees, it would only mean one thing: that we pack up and leave this land. Could it mean anything else? Why didn't Alaa answer this point honestly? Lately he used to say that this is not his problem, but rather the white man's problem. He kept calling us white! Where is he now? Where is Alaa? Ariel was angry at Alaa and this disappearance game.

There were very few cars. One would dart by and minutes would pass before another came. The sidewalks were almost empty. No elderly folks walking with their grandchildren, and no children slacking as they crossed the street. No dogs pulling their tired owners behind on their daily ritual of walking and laying a log. They walk behind their dogs and wait for them to finish to pick it up, put it in a plastic bag, and throw it in a garbage bin. Why do humans work so hard to pick up dog shit every day? Is it loneliness? Maybe he should get a cat? At last Ariel found another person walking the street.

A woman in a tight leather skirt, who looked at him as he approached as if they had a date. Despite her high heels, she was pacing elegantly back and forth between Allenby and Yavne. Her long and slender dark legs were a bit muscular. She was wearing eyeliner and her long eyelashes were so heavy with mascara they looked as if they were hugging. Her wavy orange-red hair came all the way down to her somewhat busty chest. She had a youthful face and pouty lips. She usually walked and flirted with passersby with a wink or a smile. Today there were so few of them that she appeared to be flirting with herself.

"Can I help you?" she said coquettishly.

"Yes, if you know where the Arabs have disappeared?" he answered with a sly smile.

"What's the deal? Why does everyone want to know where they disappeared?"

"It's the question of the hour."

"Why not set our own agenda for the hour, the way we like it? Like having fun together without bothering about trivial politics?"

"But if we don't know what's happening, these might be our last days here."

"What's with this obsession with Arabs and their disappearance? My pimp is an Arab and I haven't been inquiring about him. I'm standing here without protection and the son of a bitch didn't show up, but I'm going to spend the night without him. Forget about the Arabs and let's have a good time together. They'll be back. No need to worry."

She approached him, wrapped her arms around his neck, and winked as she gazed into his eyes. Her strong perfume invaded his senses and, much to his surprise, it wasn't cheap. He often saw male and female sex workers taking their spot in the area right after dark.

He took her arms off his shoulders. She was thin, but they felt heavy.

"Good night."

"Thank you, sweetie." She smiled as if certain that he'd come back. He continued to Chez George and didn't look back.

25

Chez George

He could see Chez George's dim yellow lights on the intersection of Shadal and Rothschild from afar. The place appeared far removed from all that was going on in the country that day. Ariel was surprised when the bald security guard (whose bald spot looked even brighter under the light) stopped him. Many restaurants had done away with security guards, who stood at their entrances to search bags and scrutinize the identity of those they deem suspicious. He still remembers the first time he was at a restaurant and saw that a "security" fee was added to the bill, like an indisputable tax. When did restaurants start using security guards to check bags? Was it after the second, or the first intifada? He doesn't remember exactly. He didn't dwell on it. The guard had broad shoulders and stood leaving ample space between his confident legs. The green color of his jacket bestowed some military prestige.

"What's the need for a search if the Arabs have disappeared?"

"We didn't get any new instructions."

Ariel raised his eyebrows and then his arms in the air, surrendering to the search. Then he opened and showed his bag quickly to the guard before being allowed to enter. The bar was surrounded on all four sides with burgundy leather stools. Just the night before, around this time, it was crowded with loud customers. But today there was only one couple.

"Hi Ariel."

"Hi Alex. How are you?

"Good. You?"

"Fine. Worried a bit, but good. The place is quiet today!"

"I've never seen it like that since it opened five years ago. As quiet as a cemetery. God protect us. What will happen to us?"

"What is going to happen? Things will be ok!"

"It's strange that you say this. Are you joining that chorus of those who reassure people, but without having any idea about what's going on?"

He just smiled in seeming agreement. Alex had soft chestnut hair whose ends tickled her cheeks whenever she moved or bent down to wipe the bar.

He gazed at her as if seeing her for the first time, even though he was a regular. That's a woman who loves her body, celebrates it, and wants to be desired, he thought. She never saw his eyes devouring her before the way he was doing tonight. His Arab friend is not with him tonight of course. They used to drink and talk politics and art until closing time. She thought about asking about him, but then remembered it was senseless.

Most of those who frequent the bar try, sooner or later, to flirt with Alex, even if they don't want anything. Tel Aviv is awash with desire, just as Jerusalem is awash with religious folks and with soldiers everywhere. Tel Aviv is the city of sins, as its denizens like to call it.

"Tel Aviv women are very beautiful," a German tourist once told Ariel while sitting at a café on Shenkin Street on a Friday. He stopped reading the newspaper to look at the beautiful women the German was ogling. And he told the German, "If short skirts and generous cleavage are the criteria, then they are the most beautiful in the world, without a doubt." The tourist smiled and gulped his Maccabee beer and kept ogling. Alex's voice brought Ariel back to Chez George.

"What will you drink?"

"I don't know. You know? I just don't."

"Ok, one 'I don't know' then?"

"Oh, Alex. Pugnacious as usual. A glass of the Zin I had yesterday. I think it was the 2011 . . ."

"With pleasure. What's on your mind right now?"

"You don't want to know!"

Alex smiled and made sure to look into his eyes as she poured him the wine.

"Just be honest. You have nothing to lose. This could be the last time we ever see each other. Who

knows what's going to happen? Maybe the Arabs will
crawl out of every corner like zombies and return to
exact revenge. Anything is possible. Our ancestors
never believed that we would ever have a sovereign
state, and one of the strongest armies in the world.
Who knows what our end will be like?"

"Why all this pessimism? Why do you think
the state is coming to an end? Are you one of those
who book tickets to leave and run away to Europe
or America whenever a war erupts, and only return
when it's all over!"

"No, I'm not one of them, and I only have one
passport. But I'm not one of those naïve optimists
either. I neither hate the Arabs nor love them. They
don't mean much to me. I just want them to leave us
alone. But I doubt that that's possible."

"We can't breathe or live without politics. You
asked me about what I was thinking and you forgot
the question. Instead, you give me gloomy prophecies
about the future."

He said this while looking at her cleavage. Alex
smiled and wet her lips, reciprocating his thirsty looks.

"Your eyes are gorgeous. I love that color in men's
eyes. Something in that green attracts me!"

Ariel laughed and got more comfortable in his
seat. He spread his legs and started wiggling his right
foot.

"I want you to have a drink with me, Ah Alex!"

He elongated the syllables on purpose as if kissing
each letter. She smiled and brought another glass and

poured wine for herself. She lifted it and bent forward, leaning on the bar with her left elbow.

"*Lakhayem*."

"*Lakhayem*."

Ariel extended both hands toward her and asked her to put her hands in his. He kissed her. She didn't say a word, but he felt that she was nervous. He could see her hard nipples through the black silk shirt.

"I have to finish a few things here. I have to close early tonight!"

"Why?"

"Why? Can't you see that we don't even have ten customers? It's usually packed this time. I sent most of the workers home early. We can drink something at my place later."

"Yeah, why not?"

He said while checking his text messages. Distinctive ringtones were announcing the arrival of breaking news.

"Looks like you're busy with more important things."

"No, Alex, but I'm a journalist and I have to follow the news closely in this type of situation. I felt lonely at home, so I decided to come here to write the article I have to submit. That's why I brought my laptop along. Don't take it personally."

"No worries. I understand. I have to tend to the other customers anyway. We'll talk later. The Arab workers didn't show up and I'm here with only one worker whose shift will end soon. We still have a lot to do. Clean up and see about tomorrow. I'll come back."

She smiled and Ariel noticed her dimples for the first time. He blew a kiss and she snatched it in the air with her hand and went out of the bar.

26

Ariel

It's seven thirty in the evening. He's late writing his second article. He put the earphones on and went on YouTube to find some classical music to help him concentrate. He chose a Tchaikovsky piano concerto by Barenboim. With the music in the background he surfed the sites of major newspapers to see if there was anything new. The leading article in *Yisrael Hayom* was titled "Have Our Problems Disappeared Forever?" *Yedioth Ahronoth*: "Did They Leave Until Further Notice?" He browsed through *Haaretz* more carefully and then looked at European and American newspapers. The *New York Times* had an article and an interview with an IDF officer titled "Divine Intervention by the Chosen People's Army?" He found reports and interviews about the reactions of Palestinian refugees to the news in *al-Akhbar* and *as-Safir*. Some of them reported that Palestinian refugees had attempted to infiltrate the Galilee, but there were conflicting reports about their disappearance once they crossed the Lebanese-Israeli border, as if Palestine was devouring its children. Ariel thought it was a strange simile. He moved on to other Arab news-papers, but glossed over the op-eds. All he wanted to do was make sure there weren't any news or official reactions worth mentioning, other than condemnation and disapproval.

During his army service, he learned to follow literature, popular culture, and radio and TV programs to know the general mood in the country. His superiors used to rely on whatever could be gathered in terms of data. Even after leaving the army, he kept taking the street's pulse, and used this skill in his work as a journalist. He went to his Facebook account and took a quick look. He responded to a few messages and left others unread. Many friends from all over the world were checking on him and wondering if everything was OK. He looked at the pages of some journalist friends and sent messages asking them if they had any leads or new information. He then went to the "I'm Tired of Travelling" page, which had become so popular in the last six months, it had more than 10,000 followers. Ariel was an avid follower of the page and its author, Badriyya, especially after she started going to houses in Jaffa every Thursday to collect stories for a feature she called "Our Stories. . . . From Jaffa to the World." She would knock on doors and ask people to tell her stories about Jaffa, or any other beloved city. Most preferred to talk about Jaffa. It didn't matter whether the stories were true or not, she said. History is stories and stories have histories.

Badriyya used the page to discuss social issues, too, and not just politics. She wrote once that the emotional exploitation to which parents subject their children in our societies is a form of slavery:

> When you try to settle down and pitch your tent away from the family, they start harping on the old song: "We deprived ourselves of everything so that you could study and dress well . . ." and so on. Now that is true, but does that mean I am a commodity that belongs to my parents, and I have to live the way they want, marry whom they choose, and study fields they think are best for me? In their future projections for their children, there is no failure. We are born to fulfill our parents' dreams, but I don't want to fulfill anyone's dream. Can you believe that my father is emotionally exploiting my younger brother and objecting to his fiancée, because he doesn't think her family suits ours? He tells him, "I'm not going to live much longer and I just want to be happy. I'm against this marriage. You're my only hope and I toiled to see you marry someone of your stature. This marriage will kill me." And similar things that my brother falls for. Why are young Arab men weaker than the young women? Is it because they stand to lose everything if they defy society? Or is it because they are raised to think that they are more important and they reap the material benefits of their privilege, but they are so cowardly that they cannot say to hell with material privileges?

The questions and issues Badriyya used to put on her page caused quite an uproar. Her cousin was upset and said that she was scandalizing the family by divulging details about their lives, and by revealing her personal opinions about touchy subjects, such as premarital sex, faith or lack thereof, and politics.

"That's it. We will not be silent any longer!" was the title of her last post, after the passage of the "Safety Belt" law in the Knesset. The draft law had been ratified two days before the disappearance. Is there a relation? Ariel wondered, but then cast that thought away and read Badriyya's last post.

> For all those who did not see or read the Knesset's racist fascist speech today, a full translation is provided below with my own straightforward commentary. Read for yourselves to see how we are governed by a fascist state.
>
> Prime Minister: "Ladies and gentleman. Members of the only democratic parliament in the middle east . . ."
>
> He was interrupted by one of the Arab members who yelled, "Titi, don't you read the news? What kind of a democracy is this when you are occupying another people?" The chairman struck his gavel like a butcher striking a sheep, and said to Atallah, "Atallah, if you interrupt the prime minister and disrupt the session again, I will have to order you to leave the hall."
>
> The prime minister continued his speech with a few extemporaneous words in response to Atallah:

"Had you been in an Arab country, Atallah, they wouldn't even give you the right to speak. It is our democratic state that allows those like you to speak."

A storm of applause drowned out the objections and responses from other Arab members, and those who call themselves leftists, whose numbers were dwindling. Titi continued with self-restraint:

"Esteemed Knesset members, we cannot allow the terrorists to kill democracy. When a woman goes to the doctor, and he discovers that she is afflicted with cancer, the first thing he does is treat the cancer. If the cancer has spread in the breast, he removes that breast. Otherwise, the woman's body perishes. The land of Israel is like that woman. It is threatened by cancerous cells and by those who live inside it and want to wipe it out. The law we are about to vote on is a precautionary law to protect us from the spread of this disease. I call on you to vote on this law, which stipulates that any person who doesn't celebrate our state and its independence must be deported. The security belt we have designated south of the desert is a security belt to protect us from their extremism, and from the extremism of other Arabs who are crawling from every direction. If we do not bury these cancerous cells, they will devour our bodies. They have declared war on us by invading this body, our land. It's either us or them. Either our rebirth, modernism, and democracy . . . or those who want to crush our existence, and who neither recognize it nor our independence. They talk about this thing called 'nakba' and refuse to recognize the Jewishness of this state. They have stolen our joy, victories, and even our catastrophe. The catastrophe was ours.

"It was our victory when we fought the Arabs. And our catastrophe when, like all soldiers in a war, we were forced to kill some of them. When that happened, it was a tragedy for us. We don't kill, and are not used to killing. Because our hearts are merciful and our army is ethical, we suffer even when we kill those who want to kill us. What happened in 1948 was our catastrophe, but we persevered, as we did in the past, and we built one of the strongest and most modern states in the world. It is the only democracy in the middle east. We have allowed the rest of the Arabs, who wished to remain on our land in peace, to stay here. If they want to live here, they will have to accept our conditions. Otherwise, the borders are wide open and they can go to their Arab states.

Some kind-hearted fellow countrymen are like a virus that helps the cancer spread in the patient's body, instead of removing, weakening, or controlling it. These wretched leftists, who are fooled by Arabs, say that we are building concentration camps for Arabs, like the ones the Nazis built for Jews. I say to them, if you don't put these people in the security belt camps, the representatives of al-Qaida will put you on ships and throw you into the sea. At best, they will send you back to the Europe that slaughtered us."

The hall was infused with zeal. Those elected by the people applauded the elected prime minister. The crowd was confident of everything and anything, "like triumphant lions."

Badriyya added a comment: "Had this law been passed in Honolulu, the world would have been outraged, but because it is the state of cancer, no one says a word until another holocaust takes place. And then we'll officially be the new Jews!"

Ariel looked at the comments and their time codes, especially the last one by Badriyya. It was posted at eleven the day before. He felt a lump in his throat. He used to get upset upon hearing his Arab friends' complaints and would waiver between understanding and disapproval.

27

Ariel

The Calm before the Storm?

Tel Aviv—Ariel Levy
9:15 p.m. Jerusalem

No news or war experienced by this city in the past has ever created this kind of calm. I was born and raised in Tel Aviv. I have lived here my entire life (except for three years in New York to study and work). Tel Aviv is our only fortress in the world, and we safeguard it the way we safeguard our bodies. The bodies that were hunted by Nazi Europe. Yet, our desire to live and the way we held on to it triumphed over their desire to murder us. This is our fortress, and despite having one of the strongest armies in the world, fear has not left it.

I have written a lot about Tel Aviv and have lived through many wars. I was personally affected as well; my father was killed when his chopper exploded because of a technical malfunction during the war in Lebanon. I have known fear and have lived through strange days during which we believed, even if briefly during wars, that we only had two options: life or death. As if we were reliving the fear of Masada once again. "Masada Will Not Fall Again" was and still is the slogan that sums up the general mood here. Considering how foggy things are today, this slogan is on people's minds more than ever. Everyone is on high alert. I experienced this personally before, during the two intifadas, the war in southern Lebanon, Saddam's scud-missile attack, and the wars with Hizballah and Hamas. Let alone the bus explosions. But today is different.

The city that never rests, as its denizens like to say, rested for the first time in its history. Less than an hour ago, I made a second call to a source close to the leadership of the IDF, who occupies a prominent position. A. Y. confirmed that the initial survey of all cameras in public spaces showed no irregular movement on streets. There are no congregations of Arabs, or preparations to stage demonstrations. Nor are there traces of escape attempts from prisons. The circumstances of the "disappearance" (if this is the correct term for the situation) are still not clear. This is a source of extreme embarrassment for the government and security forces in the country. Do they not know what is happening?

Initial official statements do not indicate any embarrassment, but we will see the extent of repercussions in the next few days. These events, as more than one source said to me, could lead to resignations of senior officials in the security apparatus. But we have to wait and not rush.

A state of maximum emergency was declared in the country. Leaves for government officials and the army have been suspended, and reserves have been recalled. An initial examination of hundreds of thousands of e-mails and text messages that were sent to or from Arabs in the country hasn't produced any leads as to the truth of what has taken place as of yet.

It might be speculation and not concrete knowledge to say that, regardless of the identity of the party behind it, something did happen and it was planned, but might have gone out of control. The admin of a very popular Facebook page here wrote her last post just before midnight saying, "We will not stay silent after today, and you will see." The author, Badriyya, is a resident of Jaffa. She posts regularly about events in her hometown and writes stories about the lives and concerns of her people. Badriyya's anger was palpable in her choice of words after the "Security Belt" law (aka "Precaution Law") was passed. The law stipulates that any Israeli Arab who refuses to acknowledge the independence and Jewishness of the state, or commemorates what Palestinians call "nakba" instead of independence, shall be detained. Such persons, according to the law, will be placed in a security zone the government has set up in the south until their fate is decided.

Can we extrapolate from the writings on the wall? When right-wing extremists wrote hateful remarks and issued death threats against Prime Minister Yitzhak

Rabin, God bless his soul, no one took their threats seriously. The threats, this time around, were written on a virtual wall. Social media sites have helped cause major changes in the Arab world and ushered the Arab Spring, which has turned into bloody winter. Didn't those people act after we all thought they were in eternal slumber?

What does it mean when some write, "We will not be silent anymore?" Does that mean that Palestinians will use force to realize their demands? Have they all united and planned something and outsmarted security forces? Were they able to penetrate the security barrier so easily? Or is it the exact opposite, and they all fell prey to a brilliant plan, designed by someone else, to get rid of them?

The minister of defense, possibly accompanied by the prime minister, will hold a special press conference at eleven, tomorrow morning, to appraise Israelis and the rest of the world of the latest developments. He will undoubtedly be joined by security and intelligence officials. An extensive search is underway to get to the bottom of the disappearance of Palestinians from the land of Israel. We are a few hours away from revealing the truth everyone is dying to know.

At any rate, whether Palestinians will reappear or not, what is certain is that their disappearance twenty hours ago (since the first official recorded instance was at 3 a.m.) will change things irrevocably in this country.

𝄞

Ariel relaxed in his chair and took a sip of his wine after sniffing it. He checked the news again to make sure there was nothing new before sending the article. Alex was back behind the bar and smiled when she saw him consumed by his music and writing. He smiled back without saying anything. He read the article twice, fixed a few typos, and then sent it to the shift editor in New York.

28

Rothschild Boulevard

She was standing at the intersection of Rothschild and Allenby, right where Ariel left her. After he disappeared in the distance on his way to Chez George, she went back to humming a tune thinking it would ward off a fear masked with boredom. A car slowed down and its passengers lowered their windows and started pointing and gesturing lewdly while laughing.

"*Dfokim.* Crazy sons of bitches," she muttered with a smile.

She tried to ignore them, hoping they would give up, but they didn't. They yelled at her to get in, promising to pay whatever she asked for. It didn't feel right and they wouldn't leave. One of them got out and wanted to take her by the hand to force her into the car. He went back and left the door open. Their speech was slurred and he reeked of alcohol. Dana's heart was pounding and Khamis al-Hazin was somewhere where he couldn't hear this scared heart.

She wore a fake smile as she approached the car, toyed with the driver's hair, kissed his check, and took his hand and put it on her breast.

"You go ahead to Nahlat Benyamin, across from Allenby. I'll be there in five. I just need to fix myself up."

They drove away laughing and cheering. As soon as they got far enough, she took off her high heels, and ran in the opposite direction to Chez George's.

They called her Dana, after the young Moroccan who had a sex change and became a woman and called herself Dana International. She was just Dana. With no family name, or sex change.

She doesn't know where she got her dark skin color from. Both her parents were blond. Khamis al-Hazin told her that she might be one of the stolen Yemenite children. Why didn't she have any photos of her pregnant mother? She doesn't look anything like her parents. But she didn't like Khamis's theory. It was one of those Arab myths as far as she was concerned. She looks like her maternal grandmother, whom she never saw because she died right before her birth. Assuming that all Arabs are dark, or all Europeans are blond, is silly anyway.

Passersby stop and gaze at her legs. They cannot tell for sure if she is a man or a woman. They stare at her pomegranate breasts and the bulge under her tight leather skirt (that's what she always wore).

Khamis used to tease her by asking if she put something to inflate her penis and make it bulge, or if she had one to start with. She would dare him to touch what's between her thighs to make sure. He would smile and his wide eyes would soften, but he wouldn't say anything.

"A shy pimp? When they hear you cursing, they wouldn't believe you are so tender!" Dana said laughing. Khamis al-Hazin didn't know much about Dana, except that she lived in a studio apartment on Bin Zion and that she didn't host customers. She took him to her place once when he was sick and made him tea until it stopped raining. He saw the photographs of her parents she had on the wall. She told him then that her mother had died of a heart attack. Her father was old and she couldn't take care of him because she was still too young. Khamis doesn't know how she ended up in this profession. Nor does he know why he agreed to be her pimp. He knows that money was one primary reason. Plus, working at night didn't conflict with his work hours at the bakery in Jaffa.

They chatted about politics sometimes and about how expensive things were in Jaffa, where he lives. He talked about his father's orchards, which were in limbo at Israeli courts. He didn't want to sell them, and the government refused to lift the liens on the land, which was saddled with mounds of taxes. Khamis thought it was strange that the government didn't expropriate the land. It had raped the entire country and wasn't in need of a lawful way to take things away. He would accentuate the verb "raped" whenever he spoke about the government, or anything or person he called "they." "They" always stood for the powerful ones

whose faces we never see, but we do experience the
consequences of their actions. He sent his children to
the best schools in Jaffa because he wanted them to
finish college, but he rarely saw them.

He was known to everyone as "Khamis al-Hazin."
Every Thursday morning, he would call the Arabic
section of the Voice of Israel to request Fayruz's song,
"One Day We'll Return." The first time he called,
the presenter asked him what his name was. He
said "Khamis" (Thursday). "Which Thursday?" she
asked. "Al-Hazin" (The Sad One) he said. It wasn't
clear whether this was an attribute, or his actual family name.

Khamis al-Hazin became even more famous than
the presenter. But he rejected the messages that were
sent to the station from listeners all over the Arab
world, who wanted to correspond with him. He
refused to accept messages that tried to commiser-
ate. When the presenter repeated the same question:
Why did he request "One Day We'll Return" when
he was already in Jaffa? He used to say it's because
he loved it, and longed for something he didn't quite
know. Moreover, it was the only song that made him
cry. One of the listeners wrote saying they were tired
of listening to this song, and that he had to choose
another one and stop listening to maudlin songs.
Khamis was silent when the presenter said that, then
he said:

"Alright, but if this one song is too much for
them, they can turn down the volume when it's on. I

still want to request it today and dedicate it to all our people, wherever they may be. In Syria, Lebanon, Palestine, and even in Jordan. Oh, for God's sake, let's not get into politics now. Just play 'One Day We'll Return' and I dedicate it to all the people of Jaffa, anywhere in the world."

A lie brought Khamis and Dana together. Were it not for that lie, they would've passed by each other like two parallel lines without ever intersecting. Khamis was seated at the bus stop near the intersection of Rothschild and Allenby. Winter had overstayed that year. Dana stood at the bus stop wrapped in her long gray coat, to escape the rain. A suspicious-looking man whose eyes were bloodshot approached her. He was looking sideways, as if running away from someone. He asked her if she'd seen the prostitutes who usually stand on the sidewalk. She said that she hadn't and didn't know what he was talking about.

She laughed once the man disappeared in the rain. Khamis asked her in a hesitant voice why she did. She said the man looked suspicious and, not having a pimp to protect her, she didn't want to take a chance. He smiled as he bit his cigarette to suck some smoke, and asked her why she was pimpless. The last one was a drug addict and ended up in prison. She wanted someone to protect her and not force her to do things she didn't want to do.

Dana offered him 10 percent of what she makes. She didn't know why she offered a stranger this job, and he didn't know why he accepted right away. But it was a done deal. Perhaps his strong build and the scar on his face gave the false impression that he was seasoned in the business. But that scar was a trace from childhood mischievousness and he had nothing to do with the city's underworld. His heart was softer than a butterfly's wing. But hearts are invisible. He protected Dana these past three years. The biggest challenge he faced was a shouting match. And it was solved peacefully because fate helped him. When his curses came out loud and clear in a Jaffan dialect familiar to local ears, cars came from every direction, as if they had been waiting. It seemed as if Khamis had men who protected him everywhere. This story spread and it was sufficient to give him peace of mind.

The national pastime for young Palestinian men was showing off and driving their cars at an elephant's speed in Jaffa's streets. Sometimes they used to go to the other side: to the White City. They were passing by when they heard someone shouting in Arabic. Rushing to the spot, they found Khamis screaming at a customer who had refused to pay Dana. The young men surrounded him and he and all those who had gathered around were scared. Something about Jaffans scares the denizens of Tel Aviv.

The young men would pass by every once in a while and would greet Khamis, who'd become a landmark for them. Seeing him standing there made them feel at home in that spot, which they frequented from time to time.

"*Ahlan wa sahlan*, dear. *Ahlan* brother. *Ahlayn nawwara*."

Khamis greeted back those who passed by, be they Jaffans or not, as he stood on the sidewalk in Tel Aviv, guarding Dana.

29

Chez George's

The restaurant's security guard stood like a fortified wall as soon as he saw her heading toward him. She had lifted her skirt to be able to run. As soon as she reached the restaurant she put it back down and stood.

Dana used to indicate her displeasure at the guards searching her bag by shutting it abruptly. She never believed that these measures were useful or effective. But this time she restrained herself and didn't rebuke the guard as she used to. She didn't protest or utter a word and just went in quickly. Her head swayed when she heard Edith Piaf's voice. She glimpsed Ariel at the bar so she headed there armed with a smile. He smiled back and motioned to her to join him.

"What are you doing here?"

"Working. You?"

"Taking a break from work."

"Looks like it was a quick job?"

"A bunch of losers were stalking me and I didn't want to go with them. It looked like they were wasted or high. They tried to force me into their car. I thought of calling the police, but what would they say had I told them I was a prostitute and someone was harassing me? They don't take that seriously in normal times, so imagine now? By the way, what's the latest news?"

"The latest news is that there isn't any news. Let's talk about something else."

"Like what?"

"Oh, I don't know. Are you from Tel Aviv?"

"No, Netanya, but I've been living here for ten years. Tel Aviv is the city of sins, a whore, but I love it."

Ariel laughed when he heard that.

"Where is the bartender?"

"Getting ready to close down."

Alex came back and stood like a bee behind the bar.

"*Shalom motik*. What happened? Why are you closing when it's not even midnight? Can I get a glass of wine?"

"Laila Tov! Can't you see the place is almost empty? You can still have a glass of wine, with pleasure. We're not serving food tonight, except cheese and olives."

"Black olives and wine. What kind is he having?"

"Zinfandel. Want to try it?"

"If he likes it, then I'm sure I will."

Alex poured the wine in a glass and turned around to tend to another customer on the other side who'd asked for a drink. She kept talking to him. Ariel looked her way every now and then as he was

getting ready to gather his things and put them back
in his bag.

"What do you do?"

"I'm a journalist. A correspondent for an American newspaper."

"Do you like your job?"

"Most of the time. You?"

Dana laughed when she heard his question.

"No. But I learn to like it every night as I do it. I'll
stop in two years. I'm tired, frankly. I'm tired and we
don't get any younger . . ."

"No, we don't. But who knows? Maybe we won't
even have the chance to get older. Who knows what
tomorrow has in store for us?"

"Ah. What will it have? Everything will be fine.
Frankly, after all these years of work and toil I don't
want the world to end tomorrow. I want to live a
little longer and enjoy life. Why are you being so
serious?"

"You're right. I don't know. *Lakhayem.*"

"*Lakhayem motik.*"

"And what do you want to do once you retire?"

"I'll try to open a small café, but that'll be difficult in Tel Aviv. I don't want to go back to Netanya.
And if I want to open the type of café I have in mind,
no place other than Tel Aviv would be suitable. I have
some money saved. Enough to open a Berlin-style
café and restaurant. You know? I was there a while
ago and they have a lot of new cafés and restaurants
that offer simple food, but the décor is funky. Maybe

I'll look for an Arab house that I can fix up and do something similar. We'll see. I also want to have a steady relationship, to be in love, but my work doesn't allow that."

"A lovely project. I hope you succeed. I'll be one of the customers if all goes well after these events."

"We'll see. *Lakhayem*, again."

Ariel gestured to Alex, who'd come to stand next to them. She raised her glass and, after taking a sip, said in an icy tone:

"I have to close in fifteen minutes."

"Understood. Can we get the bill then?"

"It's on me." Ariel said looking at Dana and smiling.

"*Toda motik. Ata* gentleman."

"A glass of wine won't deplete my budget. Plus, I ate more than half of the olives."

"Want to come for a drink at my place?" Alex said, looking at him with anticipation in her voice, but he hesitated.

"Honestly, I'm very tired and have a lot on my mind. I can't focus except when writing my articles and I have to. I don't want to come to your place for the first time and be in such a sorry state. And I have to get up early."

He took her hand and kissed it, but she withdrew it quickly with an extinguished smile.

"OK, darling, I hope your head clears up."

"I want to come, but it's a tough tonight. Do you understand? I'll stop by some other night soon."

Alex didn't say more and started collecting her stuff. Dana looked at Ariel and said in a hushed voice, "Looks like you ruined this night and your chances for coming nights with this beautiful woman."

He smiled and raised his eyebrows. They waited for Alex to go out to the street all together.

30

A Man and a Memory

Dayan was more than eighty and his hair was hoary, but neither his memory nor his health were weak. Shock turned him into a statue watching TV. He couldn't believe what he had heard and seen on Channel 1: empty houses and ghost streets in Arab neighborhoods.

Did he lose the opportunity forever? Why had he waited and never knocked at the door of that house? It was only ten minutes away by car. What will he do now? Will the catastrophe be repeated? It wasn't a catastrophe for him. Were it not for the pinpricks of his persistent conscience, things would be fine.

Thoughts swirl in his head like a trapped fly that keeps hitting the glass of a shut window. His thoughts keep him awake at night. For more than sixty years now he's been waking up many a night, drenched in his sweat. He sees her as clear as day and still remembers that night. The Arabs had decided that they didn't want them. Could they have lived here any other way? He repeated those thoughts and then voiced them out loud, as if fearing they would escape.

163

A thread of doubt about that night revisits him every now and then.

What could he possibly say about what took place? That night hunts him. He wanted to apologize, just to get it off his chest, and rest; maybe she would too. But who says she's tired. She must be? No? He should have gone to that accursed house a long time ago, but he couldn't. Her silence hunted him. What he did that night hunts him. He feels that everything around him is not his. No, he doesn't feel that, but something around him is not his. Something disturbs his happiness. He should have gone to her house. To say what? She has been sitting in front of her house every day and grinding the mortar for more than sixty years saying, "I chose you, Hasan." Is Hasan her husband? Where did he go? What can he do? He asked a young Arab he knew to accompany him, and stay close to her to listen and translate what she said. She spoke of many things he couldn't understand. He didn't know if the translation was bad or there was some other reason. What does "I chose you, Hasan" mean? Who is Hasan? These Arabs say many meaningless things. He sighed deeply as if this last thought had appealed to him more than before. Yes, yes, these Arabs talk a lot. But why can't he forget? Why did she have to go now, before he could talk to her?

Sometimes he dreams that he is tongue-tied and he cannot untie his tongue. He sees himself inside his mouth trying to untie his tongue. He speaks in the dream even when he's tongue-tied and no one understands what he says. He cannot take the night-mare within the nightmare. It disappears for a long period, only to return and haunt him again. When he joined the organization they told him they were defending the last spot they had left in the world. What can he do today? He survived everything except that black place in his memory, which is stuffed with nightmares. It grinds him from time to time. He didn't want to be weak. Maybe he hated the Arabs because they were weak like him. No, no one is like them. He will say that what happened to them never happened before, nor will it happen again. He didn't want to do that, but they forced him. And he didn't say no!

It was raining, unusual for springtime. They had "cleaned" one of the neighborhood in al-Lid. That's what they termed what they did. Dayan didn't go into the houses with them. He stayed at the beginning of the street with the others who guarded the entrance to neighborhoods. Moteh told him that cleaning was only meant to scare the Arabs, nothing more. "We have to show them our fangs. We don't want Israel to become another Europe." He didn't ask what "clean-ing" meant.

It was raining heavily on the way back to Tel Aviv from al-Lid. Moteh said he was hungry and what he'd eaten in al-Lid was not enough. Dayan didn't under-stand what he meant. Moteh said that the Pin gang was in Jaffa that night. He was going and they all had to go along. Everyone agreed. He was afraid to ask.

He tried to leave and claimed he was tired, but how can a fighter claim to be tired? Do fighters ever tire?

They went to house no. 10 on Ayn Street in Jaffa. The address was carved in his memory, because Moteh kept repeating it, as if it were a song. It was a beautiful house with three rooms, yellowish stone walls. On that rainy night, guards from the Pin gang stood outside. They only let in those who were part of the group and knew the password. When he went in, he stumbled on a flowerpot. There were many of them throughout the courtyard and the guestroom. He still remembers the sound of rain falling that night. It was knocking at the high windows.

When they walked into the house they saw a spacious room with a carpet and a man in the middle. Was it this Hasan she keeps calling? He was lying facedown to the floor, and his pants were down to his knees. Moteh said, "Whoever wants to should go ahead. Come! His dark ass is tight. If you don't like the tail, there is a woman's hole next door." Dayan couldn't believe his eyes. One of them slapped him teasingly. Moteh took Dayan by the hand to the room next door. She was there crying. Her skinny body was naked and they were taking turns.

"Why are you standing there like an idiot? Aren't you a man? Go ahead and show her who the real men are. Go on, I said . . ."

He moved forward quietly and didn't say anything. As if he were numb. He wanted to be numb. He stood before her, looking at her skinny body. She was weeping. Moteh moved closer and screamed at her to stop crying and laugh instead. To call out to him and say, "Come, I want you." If she didn't do that he was going to take her out to the street and fuck her in front of everyone. That's what he said. She opened her eyes, and looked into their faces, and spat at him. Moteh struck her on the face and told Dayan, "Show her." She didn't scream. Why didn't she? Had she screamed, they might've stopped raping her. She did scream a bit, but they stopped her.

He no longer remembers whether she screamed or not. As if her voice couldn't exit her throat. Her eyes were full of fear. "Fear" wouldn't be the exact word. They were full of horror. When Moteh lowered Dayan's pants, yelled at him that he has to be a man, he lay over her, pretending to have an erection. He was moving on top of her. He could smell the odor of the bodies that had taken turns. He didn't smell her scent. They stood around her laughing and saying that his ass was snow white. "Show this Arab. Show her!" said Moteh again, his laugh like cawing.

They left the house. Later he learned that she didn't escape and had decided to stay. He doesn't know if the man died or what became of him. Perhaps he was still there, but he didn't see him. Moteh said he didn't want to kill them. He wanted them to live to tell the others so that fear would spread among them.

She stayed there saying things in Arabic that no one understood. She sat outside the house every day talking to herself or to passersby. She never looked people in the face. Always looking at the sea. He would pass by but stay at a distance. He sees her, but she doesn't see him. Perhaps she does, but doesn't want to see him. He passes by and thinks of going up to her and apologizing, but he cannot do it. What good will it do? His voice stays muffled in his throat. As if it is her voice, muffled inside his own throat. The voice that never comes out. Maybe it does, but he cannot hear it. What will he do today if she disappears like the rest? To whom will he apologize? To whom? Her voice is a shard of glass standing in his throat:

I chose you, Hasan . . .

I chose you, Hasan . . .

I chose you, Hasan . . .

The sentence and her voice in his throat haunts him. A shard of glass. Her voice is a shard of glass. Tonight, he hears it clearly for the first time in so long. He hears her voice clearly tonight. Is it her voice he is hearing? He hears a voice . . . a voice made of glass shards.

31

Ariel

Ariel kissed Alex, who was still cold with him, on the cheek, and promised her to come back in the following few days. He went out with Dana and said goodbye at the door and then walked back to his apartment. He looked for the building number before turning around. As if wanting to make sure that building no. 45 of the restaurant was still there, and he wasn't dreaming or delirious. He went the other way. When he reached no. 16, he sat on the wooden bench in front of the building and scrutinized the statue of the man on the horse. He looked at Dezingoff House, which was now a museum. It was a modest building and he remembered the simple furniture he saw inside when he visited to see the place where Ben Gurion established this tiny dream and declared independence. He got up and headed toward the building. He climbed the nine steps and touched the door. Who could've imagined that they could return after thousands of years? He smiled at the thought. It was a long road across all these continents, but there was no other way. Yes, that's what his English

paternal grandfather wrote in his memoirs when he
came here in the 1920s. He was a real "gentleman"
and believed in the importance of western European
Jews saving their brethren in eastern Europe from
anti-Semitism. This was the only place where no one
would threaten them. After their arrival, their Arab
neighbors got water and electricity and the number
of orange groves in Jaffa doubled. It's true the Jaffans
had developed the Shammuti oranges eighty years
before, and that Jaffa oranges were a registered trade-
mark before Herzl thought of Zionism. His grandfather never denied that, but the knowhow brought by
men and women who came from established empires
is what developed the country. He's not a colonizer.
He was returning to his ancestors' land after thousands of years. That's what his grandfather wrote in
his memoirs. He said that any progress Palestine witnessed was European, French, or English. The rail-
road, for example, was French. His ancestors came
from these civilizations. That's what his grandfather
wrote, and what his father used to say when they dis-
cussed politics. Ariel reminded himself of all that. He
wasn't naïve enough to believe everything his grandfather wrote, but he knows that they are alike, somehow. Ariel takes pride in his grandfather, the able
English Zionist who came to the promise land. He
was English in everything, but he adopted Zionism.
It became more than an idea, but rather a way of life.
He believed in it like a warrior. His grandfather saw
Palestinians as nomads and peasants, passersby and

no more. Unlike some Zionists of his generation, he never wrote that he was in favor of expelling Palestinians. He wanted to buy as much land as possible. It's true that the land that was sold was not much, no more than 10 percent. But what is important is that they were able to control it and build this miraculous western country in the heart of a backward east. It was a war, and they won. He cannot see things any other way, Ariel thought. He resisted any thought that would doubt the veracity of what his grandfather had said. Yes, his grandfather was English, but he was no colonizer. He cannot call him a colonizer even if there is a resemblance. Ariel held on to that thought as if he didn't want it to leave his mind.

He took a deep breath as he looked at the avenue. The building stood quietly that night. Although it was not that famous, it did witness a miraculous resurrection. He smiled and headed to the sea instead of going back to his apartment, but he didn't take the short way. He made sure to go back and pass through some of the streets that intersect with Rothschild. He felt the need to breathe in the place and the history of the White City on the path he chose to the sea.

32

Ariel

The memory of white, and the memory of black. Does a place have memory? What if we were to place a person who knew nothing of the place's history, not even its name or geographic location. If we were to take him, and have him walk in the city or place, would he feel the place's memory? Which memory? Ariel wondered this while remembering arguments he had with Alaa about this subject. He was looking at street signs and names. He was counting the important landmarks of the avenue: the architecture, houses, and stories he had read or heard. This city has the largest number of Bauhaus buildings, the style fascism banned. Bauhaus found its freedom here: creative architecture, whose philosophy broke free from complexity to combine form and function. This style of architecture found a home in this tiny country after it fled fascist Europe, Ariel thought as he looked at the buildings. But he couldn't hide his admiration of the ones designed by Yehuda Magidovitch, whose original style one recognizes in many houses on Rothschild. Ariel laughed when he remembered the story he read about Churchill's visit, and how Dezingoff, then the mayor, took big old trees from adjacent areas and spread them around so they would appear as if they had been there for a lifetime. But one tree fell down and embarrassed him. Laughing, Churchill said, "Without roots nothing will grow here." Ariel imagined Churchill's laugh and heard it roaming the avenue, but he wondered about the veracity of this story.

When he reached the intersection of Rothschild and Balfour he remembered how Alaa once told him that he felt someone was whipping him when he walked and saw these street names. He said he had memorized the map by heart without names, so he wouldn't look at street signs. Sometimes he took the longer way home so as not to go through streets whose names whipped him. Was Alaa a prisoner of the past? Why all this thinking about the past?

On one of his visits to Alaa's apartment, Ariel found a large number of signs of street names that Alaa had removed and brought home. He'd painted them over in black and wrote other names on them in green. He crossed out "Rothschild" and called it "Sharabi Street." He loved Hisham Sharabi, had read everything he had written, and believed that he deserved to have a wide street named after him.

Was Ariel's mistake that he sometimes listened to Alaa and tried to understand him when he spoke about these things? Why couldn't Alaa just enjoy living in a modern state with all this freedom anyway?

He remembered how Alaa erupted in anger when he heard him say that. Ariel told him he understood that mistakes were made, and that Palestinians needed more rights, but he had to acknowledge that this state gave him so much. His situation is much better than the refugees in Lebanon, for example, or Arab countries. Alaa laughed out hysterically.

Ariel was crossing the intersection of Balfour and Ehud Ha'am and felt a certain anger within. He wondered out loud, "Where are you, Alaa? What did you want? That we change 'Ehud Ha'am' and call the street 'al-Qassam'? You should've stayed. Perhaps the day will come and you can then change whatever you want. Where are you now? What kind of game is this?"

"Shut up you son of a bitch. We want to sleep," said an angry voice coming from an open window on a ground floor apartment. Ariel shot back, "Go to hell. You are the son of a bitch," and continued toward Allenby.

Night itself was awake, as if it, too, was waiting to know what had happened. It was past one o'clock in the morning, but many of the lights in the houses he was passing were still lit.

Ariel walked Feierberg, Melchett, Ayn Fered, and Straus streets, as if leafing through pages in a book. His thoughts reached out to touch street names as if honoring the persons who brought this city into being from nothing. Yes, we arose out of nothing, didn't we? What was here before except orange groves and villages?

Ariel recalled how Alaa once erupted in a spot nearby when he asked him to stop saying this was Jaffa and its villages. He told him that he had to be a forward-looking, modern person, and not let the past hold him back. Many cities are destroyed and are rebuilt. He should look forward, if he wants to catch up. Alaa was furious like never before and screamed:

"You've never heard of al-Manshiyye, Shaykh Muwannis, il-Mas'udiyyeh, and all of Jaffa's villages? What does it mean for me to be modern? To just bend over for you to violate me while I applaud you? When will you understand that Tel Aviv is the lie that everyone believed? By the way, Jaffa wasn't just groves! Even if it was just desert, this lie you all wanted to believe doesn't grant you the right to kill us and expel us. Even if we were the most backward people in the world, that doesn't give you the right to displace us. Nor to kill us. Go and fight the Europe which expelled you and killed you . . ."

While Alaa kept yelling at Ariel, some passersby had stopped.

"Let's go now. No need for these comparisons. It's painful."

"I'm not comparing. What comparison? I listen and listen and listen. You guys talk all the time and we listen. We try to get you to understand that something is wrong in the equation. Sometimes we try to speak quietly, and we often stay silent. We are afraid and get upset. We hate you and get close to you or love you as humans. We mimic you and believe you, but we know that we are lying to ourselves, first and foremost. We tell ourselves they will understand, but you don't listen to us. Everything we say is lost in translation. Even when we speak the same language. We realize that nothing will make you listen to us and hear us unless we scream at you. Unless we throw our drizzle in your faces so you stop and hear what we are saying."

"What do you want now?" Ariel asked in anger, but Alaa didn't pay attention and yelled at those who had gathered around.

"If you don't gather the wreckage of what you broke, these shards will explode in your faces even if you bury them underground and build above them. Why are you looking at me as if am crazy? Palestinians will return from every corner. Your nightmare will come true, unless you hurry up and burn us all and finish everything. You can cry for us after that."

One of those who had surrounded Alaa yelled as he was coming forward confidently,

"What are you talking about you idiot? We returned to our land. You are the occupiers. Go to the Arab countries!"

Ariel pulled Alaa away saying, "We have to go. We have to go before they eat you alive."

They didn't talk for two weeks after that incident, and they avoided talking about politics, or at least about the place's history and memory.

Ariel reached the end of Allenby. The opera building was on his right and the sea in front of him. He
turned left and walked along the beach to Tsfoni
Café, his favorite place on the beach. Alaa loved it
too. They used to meet there to chat, drink beer, and
swim.

He greeted the waiter who appeared to have just
finished smoking a joint and had a stupid smile on
his face. The café had chairs and tables directly on
the beach where he liked to sit. There were only three
customers sitting at a table, playing cards. He didn't
take much time to decide where to sit. He took off his
shoes and walked on the sand toward the first row of
plastic chairs. He settled into the chair. Nothing but
darkness and the sea before him. He toyed with the
sand with his right foot.

Would the Palestinians have developed the place
like this had they established their own state? Ariel
wondered as he looked at the timid lights of Jaffa on
his left. What if the state hadn't been established?
What if we didn't gain independence and they had
their Palestine? What would've happened? How
would this country be? How would we be? He felt the
need to look behind to the giant buildings extending
along the beach.

He moved closer to the big lamp next to his table
and took out the red notebook from his bag and put it
on the table. Before starting to read, he looked at his
cell phone. No one had called in the last three hours.
He felt at peace. He ordered a cheese sandwich and

local beer for the first time in a while. He picked up the red notebook. He forgot the page he'd folded so he leafed through and settled on a random page. He leaned back in his chair, brought the lamp closer, and gazed at the sea before beginning to read.

33

Alaa

I remember the beginnings of love well, but I don't remember its end. Does love end? Was it love, or its disappointment, that prevented you from remarrying? Do you remember how I used to call you by your first name, "Huda," instead of Tata when I was a child? Something in you kept insisting on life and on hope, so much so that it made you tired. You were like Jaffa. It became a city made of spider cobwebs: elastic, flexible, and transparent. But they are well-knit, strong, and come back to being. Do you know how a spider builds its web? We are just like it. I see us resembling it. I see you as a female spider, you and all those who stayed in Jaffa. I have a powerful will to live, even if it tires me at times, and I think I inherited that from you.

You asked me once why I didn't get married. I didn't know how to answer. I told you there was no luck. But the truth is there is a question that hovers around me. Why would I bring other Palestinians to this world? Aren't there enough wretched Palestinians on this earth already?

Is this the real nakba? I don't see myself ever committing suicide. That seems to me the natural thing any normal human would do, because what we see around us in this world is intolerable.

But I don't commit suicide. So, have I inherited your spider talents, but I weave my webs differently? Or is that a lie I tell myself to find a reason to live?

My excuses were the failed love stories I lived. I'm still looking. I still acclimate after each love story. The ones that crushed my heart weren't many. It was crushed and withered twice. But it sprang back to life. Other than that, they were mostly beautiful but passing ones.

Do you remember Raghda? The first time I saw her she was sitting with Nabih at the cafeteria of the College of Humanities at Tel Aviv University. She laughed out loud at his jokes and didn't pay attention to anyone around her. Her orange shirt accentuated her dark skin and full chest. I didn't like those who wore light and bright colors, but that shirt was beautiful. She was soft, slender, and young when I first met her. She was maybe twenty or twenty-one, but was liberated and relaxed. Her honesty is what attracted me the most. I liked her coal-black hair. She didn't wear much makeup, except some light kohl around her big eyes.

I remember the night I told her about my feelings. I was very nervous and was surprised because I had gone out with other women and Raghda wasn't a stranger. We'd become friends and met many times

alone or with that strange group I was part of back
then. We agreed to meet at a fish restaurant on the
beach. I went early to reserve a spot on the balcony
overlooking the sea.

She came wearing tight jeans with a sleeveless
black shirt. My heart melted when I saw her walking
in black high heels. I melted into her beautiful coffee-colored eyes. "Beautiful" doesn't do them justice.
Enchanting. That's a better word . . .

We talked about politics, the country, relationships, people, and about Jaffa, of course. I told her
about you. I used to tell everyone I met about you.
About what it means to become the orphan of a country while you're still in it. That's how I see you. We
talked a lot and time passed by quickly. We were
the last customers and it was very hot. I craved her
intensely and was afraid to tell her about my feelings.
But I knew the situation was favorable. All the other
tables were empty. The sea was peaceful and charming
that night. I got up and took three candles from the
tables next to us and put them on ours. She laughed
and said, "You're so romantic." Her puffy lips were
glimmering and the wine had made them red.

I was about to speak, but the cunning waiter's
voice, as if he were the grim reaper, asked us if we
wanted anything, because it was last call. I asked for
a brandy and she stayed with red wine. After he came
back with the drinks, I moved and sat in the chair
next to her. I took a sip of the brandy and started to
kiss her, giving her half of the sip and biting her lips.

She smiled, moved a little, and we laughed a lot. I kissed her passionately again. Perhaps you are clearing your throat and saying, "That's enough, grandson. I'm your grandmother not your friend. No need for all these details." But you used to say that Jaffans love life, love, and flirting.

The night she left me I felt as if a hurricane had stormed the city. "We can't get married," she said, lying next to me in bed and gazing at the cloudy sky through my dorm room window at Tel Aviv University. My roommate had gone to visit his family in the north and Raghda and I spent the weekend together. We never left the room except to go to the bathroom or open the door for food delivery. We spent the weekend listening to Um Kulthum, reading poetry, and chatting, then waking up to fall back asleep again.

"Why can't we get married? We can go to Cyprus and get married there. Your family is open-minded and they won't mind. I can persuade my family. We'll live in cities and our friends and the people around us don't give a damn about religion."

"Alaa, my family won't agree and I don't have the energy to fight a backward society. What about children?"

"Since when do you care about these things, Raghda? Unbelievable."

"I don't, but I can't cause my dad all these problems."

She didn't give me a chance to convince her to change her mind. She decided on behalf of both of us.

We had been together for a year and a half. I would suffocate when she was away. Maybe she was right. Maybe. Because this society is merciless. No, she wasn't right. But she would've had to sacrifice much more in the end merely because she is a woman. She left Tel Aviv after finishing her studies and went back to the Galilee and got married. We kept in touch, but with time, it was meaningless. I used to ask about her from time to time and I learned that she had a daughter she called Amal.

My second love story, which didn't end like fairy-tales do, was with Jumana. I've never seen anyone in my life who worked, stayed up late, slept, went out, ate, read, danced, and loved voraciously the way she did. She was brilliant and insane. I was very happy with her, but she was the most miserable person I ever met. I knew at a certain point that our relation-ship would not endure, because she couldn't stay in the country and I had no desire to immigrate. The last week I saw her she had returned after a ten-day vacation to see her family. She was sad and not her-self, as if her spirit had been stolen from her. I tried to understand what had happened, but she didn't say much at first. Then, all of a sudden, she said she wanted to leave the country. She was sick and tired of both Arabs and Jews, and of Palestine and all things Palestinian. She got a scholarship to complete a doc-torate in comparative literature in London. She said I shouldn't wait for her because she didn't know if she would return to this grave. Yep, she called the

country a "grave." I never saw her since and I don't
know if she ever returned, even for a visit. I asked
about her more than once, but she'd cut everyone off.
I sent her letters, but her replies were very abrupt. I
realized she wanted nothing to do with me, or this
country. She went as if she never existed.

Why am I telling you all this? Because you were
the only one in the family that talked openly about
sex, life, and marriage. You used to say that the people of the Jaffa you had known used to talk about
relationships and life unabashedly.

I wish an older and more experienced person had
given me some advice. My father never did that. My
mother seems to have lost her sense of motherhood
when she had the hysterectomy, which she never talks
about. She only did once when I asked her why she
never had another child. She said it in a very cold
manner.

My parents were running around to compensate
me for something, but they forgot the simplest things.
When we are teenagers we think that no one understands us or our situation. So, we refuse to talk to our
family about the details of our life, thinking that they
are backward and won't understand us. We move out
and away from home when we are older. We choose
to study and live somewhere else, far removed from
anything related to our family. When we mature, we
realize, often belatedly, that we can actually talk to
them about our problems. But by then they are gone.
I wish you'd stayed longer. I wish I'd learned to talk

more to my parents. You know that after you died my relationship with my dad improved. Still, something prevents me from talking to them at length about my feelings. As if am punishing them for not giving me that opportunity when I was still young.

What can I say? My father chose his death. I don't think it is bad in and of itself. He was about to go blind and didn't want to live like that, so he put an end to his own life. What bothers me is the sadness he must have felt when he made that decision. What saddens me is that he didn't love us enough to stay for us. Am I so selfish to think of his love for us or lack thereof and not . . . Maybe he committed suicide because he didn't wish to be a burden to anyone? He wanted to leave us while he was still the way he always was. Saying very little, working, reading, and travelling a lot. And being alone somehow. Didn't I already say that survivors are the loneliest?

I feel very sad when I remember him and remember you. Is there life after death? I don't know. You believed that there is. If so, then why don't you appear to me? Why don't you come visit me from time to time? Maybe you come when I don't think of you? Maybe you are present and all I have to do is look beyond the glass that surrounds me. The glass that I live behind to protect myself from hearing and smelling what I don't want to. How else would I be able to live here? I firmly believe now that all those who stayed in Palestine are mad. Otherwise how would they be able to bear the memory of those who survived, and those who didn't? How can they live with this pain in the memory of the survivors?

Do you remember when I came once and you were alone? I had never seen you carrying so much sorrow before then. When I asked you what was wrong, you said that staying in Palestine after the nakba *is* being orphaned. To stay in Jaffa is to be an orphan. "I was remembering Prophet Rubin's feast and how we used to go there and how everything changed. As if Palestine collapsed over our heads . . . Jaffa collapsed over our heads. Why did that happen? I don't know . . . What did we do? No use now, everything has a bitter taste. We have to make sweets out of what is sour. Feast *ka'k* have become bitter. Sugar became bitter and, by God, all that remains is this sea . . . We are orphans, grandson, orphans."

Longing for her is like holding a rose of thorns!

Longing is thorns.

34

Alaa

I'm tired, tired, tired. But then I say again that this is my only chance to live and I have to live it. You will be angry and say that am still young. How can I be young when my hair has become white? Yesterday I saw Abu Muhsin, our neighbor. Do you remember him? I swear I think he was in love with you. I was in Ajami looking for paint for your house. I'm moving there. I didn't tell you before, but I've decided to fix the house and live in it, so I can be closer to mother. The twenty houses separating your house from hers will be enough space for me to have my privacy, but still be close enough so she won't feel lonely. You know she started to go on trips outside Jaffa? Oh, yes, since father's death she's been going with a group of women to the Dead Sea, or Tiberias, and some other places too. They stay for a night or two and she comes back reinvigorated. They laugh a lot, she said. She tells me about many people whose names I don't know and tells their jokes and pranks. They rent a tiny bus and go on a trip on their own. "Sweet," is all

I said. I find the smile that stays on her face long after she comes back from these trips strange.

Anyway, I went to paint your house and I sat with Abu Muhsin on the steps of his house. His granddaughter, Naziha, made us coffee. Abu Muhsin is tired of life, too, but life doesn't want to leave him. That's what he said.

"This life is stuck and stamped unto me and doesn't want to let go . . . Ah, Alaa, I really miss your grandmother. I'm tired and this God of yours doesn't want to take his servant. Do you know that Abu Mazin died?"

He said it as the sun was departing.

"Which Abu Mazin? Do you mean Mahmoud Abbas?"

"No, man. Our old neighbor, Abu Mazin. They took his land after 1948 and forced him to work on it. Can you believe the humiliation?"

"May God have mercy on his soul and may he grant you long life."

"If God wanted to be merciful to him, he would've been so while the man was still alive. Maybe the grave is much better than living in this grave of a life!"

"Come on, man. Take it easy and be optimistic."

"Optimistic, shoptimistic! That's just useless bullshit. These Israelis are motherfuckers and they'll never leave us alone. When they came to this country they wanted to finish us off. You know I lived through all that humiliation. There is no other solution. Either they finish us off, or we finish them off.

Because they're not willing to live with us, or just let us live."

"What are you talking about, Abu Muhsin? Not all Israelis are the same. There are good Israelis and bad ones. There were betrayals and massacres. But still, they weren't all OK with what happened. And frankly, we made mistakes too. Moreover, the victim should not lose its moral high ground. Plus, what are we going to do to the Israelis who were born here? Just throw them out one day if you have the power?"

"Man, I don't want to get into this smart educated talk and bullshit. Whoever wants to liberate Palestine let them roll their sleeves. You want to be an intellectual now? What about all those refugees who left? That's it for them? Who says so? Even God couldn't say that. But I'm not talking about the refugees. I'm talking about the Israelis who are fucking us over. It's not like they even accept being part of this region and acknowledge what happened and we're rejecting that. They're making our lives hell and they keep crying. They have one of the strongest armies in the world and they keep saying we are so helpless and the whole world is against us . . ."

"And what's the solution?"

"There isn't. Just like Nasser said, 'What was taken by force can only be taken back by force.'"

"We don't want the force of weapons. We want another type of power."

"Oh, son, you're still dreaming, and you still believe in that stuff? How did they fool us? You know

what, let them accept the one-state solution and recognize our rights and allow the refugees to return.
Who would say no to that? You're giving me a headache. I want to go eat and sleep. I have to wake up
too fuckin' early to work. God have mercy on your
grandmother."

🌾

Ariel stopped reading and closed the notebook. He
felt a headache in his temple that radiated slowly to
the rest of his body. He was tired of reading Alaa's
stories and of the past and the endless talk about
the place and its memory. These are the tales of the
defeated about the myths of the past. Yes, that's what
they are. He looked long at the sea. Everything was
calm around him. Even the sea was calm. Is it divine
intervention? He wondered and smiled, mocking
himself for thinking that. Where did they go?

"Do you want another drink?"
"No, thanks. The bill please?"
"Eighty shekels!"
"Toda Raba. Keep the rest."
"Toda. Leila Tov."
"Leila Tov."

35

Ariel

Is the fear he feels now that same fear his father felt in 1967, six days before Ariel was born? The fear of total destruction by the fall that could've become a fall to the abyss? But that fear was followed instead by ecstasy. His father told him, "We shocked the Arabs on that day, six days before you were born. We thought they were going to throw us into the sea for sure. They would attack us from all sides. But the great surprise was when we discovered that this young country, only nineteen years old back then, didn't only defend itself fiercely, but somehow became a tiny empire. The ecstasy of victory was unparalleled, and then you came." Ariel remembers his father's words very well. He used to return to that reservoir, his chest of memories, whenever he felt his confidence in what was taking place becoming shaky.

He rarely harbored any doubts. He did, once, back when he served in the army. He remembers the terrified faces of Palestinians when they used to surround their homes in the middle of the night to arrest their children and take them to interrogate them. Some of

them were so young and he never understood where
they got all that stubbornness from. He recalled those
looks from time to time after finishing his military
service, and when he returned for reserve service in
later years.

They were watching a youth standing next to
someone his age, throwing rocks at them. "Look at
this aggressive mouse throwing rocks at us," said his
colleague. "I'll show him," he added, as he looked
at the "mouse" through the scope. Snipers were like
gods. With a pull on the trigger they decided who
could stay alive and who would be expelled from it.

Ariel and two fellow soldiers approached the
young man whom the soldier's finger had decided
should fall. When they were close, his breath was still
warm. "What brought you here?" Ariel yelled at the
corpse. "He's a boy. Not yet fourteen," Ariel screamed
into the mic that carried his voice to the ear of the soldier who had pulled the trigger. "He didn't look that
young from behind the trigger," said the sniper.

The dead youth's friend stood a hundred meters
away, his hands full of rocks. He didn't flee. Fear died
inside him and he froze. When Ariel apprehended
him to deliver him to be interrogated, he had to drag
him to the jeep. He kept looking at his friend's corpse
as the jeep was pulling away. He didn't shed a single
tear and stayed silent. It was a cold silence.

36

Ariel

He shook the dust off his feet, put his shoes on, and carried his black bag on his left shoulder. There was a heavy presence of police cars and a large number of tanks and military vehicles heading north on the main street.

He saw three buses full of settlers, heading south to Jaffa, pass in front of him. What will they do now? Will they turn against secular citizens? The spectacle worried him. Using his cell phone, he searched the internet for any news about the subject. He walked along the shore from Tel Aviv to Jaffa to catch up with them and see what was going on.

He stood in front of the Hasan Beg Mosque, which was by the shore on his left. The Ottoman style of the building, which was surrounded by all these luxury hotels, looked conspicuous and incongruous. Do the hotel residents ever wonder about the mosque? He crossed the street to the other side. The mosque's outer gate and its door were both shut. He looked at the security camera hanging above. He climbed the iron gate, jumped over, and landed on

his right foot. He felt a slight pain as he climbed the
steps and tried the door handle, but it was locked. He
shook it and knocked forcefully. He waited a bit and
then put his left ear closer to the door. He thought he
heard a rattle. He tried to open the door again. He
went down the steps and went around. Why did he
stop here? A beautiful building can be built in this
huge courtyard without demolishing the old mosque,
he thought. It can be left there. It might happen soon.
He looked again in Jaffa's direction. He called the
army's media office, which had announced earlier
that it would stay open twenty-four hours in the coming days. He inquired about a response to his request
to accompany the army as they enter Arab houses in
Jaffa. They assured him that his request had not been
processed yet, and they would e-mail him as soon as
a decision was made, probably in the next few hours.
He put his cell phone back in his pocket. He climbed
the main gate to exit the mosque and walked toward
Jaffa. He waved to the few cars passing by, hoping
that someone would stop and give him a ride to the
next intersection. A police car stopped and asked him
what he was doing outside at that hour and in these
circumstances. He identified himself and asked the
policeman to take him along. The policeman hesitated, but then agreed to take him to the main square.

37

At the Gates of Umm al-Gharib

He remembered that interview he had conducted with one of the settlers from Ofra, the first settlement in Judea and Samaria, as he calls the West Bank most of the time. He wondered if one of them is there. He was surprised that he enjoyed talking to the settlers. He appreciated their love for the place and their notion about the importance of Zionist presence on the land of biblical Israel. He understood what they wanted, but he still had disagreements with them. They believed that the modern state cannot be complete without a soul and a spiritual life. And they were the soul of this state by settling the promised land. He wrote an article back then based on those interviews and was criticized by some because its tone was receptive to the settlers. However, despite not agreeing that their presence there is necessary, he saw them as farmers, determined to fulfill a dream that lived for more than three thousand years. He held on to that idea as he sat in the back seat of the police car trying to see the buses heading to Jaffa. The road took less than five minutes. The policeman didn't want to make small talk, and Ariel wasn't persistent in his questions.

The incoming settlers' buses were blocking the entrance to the main square. Ariel stood behind the throngs at first, watching the spectacle. Then he moved forward slowly. Most of them were young, some pale, others were combing their long beards, as if preparing to devour their prey.

"Good morning all. Good morning to our free and sacred land. We have arrived in Jaffa and our brethren in Jerusalem are standing outside many houses there to enter as soon as the army allows us to do so there and elsewhere in the promised land."

Voices thanking God for his grace billowed, chief among them that of their red-cheeked, soft-spoken leader. His white shirt and blue blouse couldn't totally hide the excessive fat he carried. His graying beard bestowed some solemnity.

"What is important now is that I hope you don't clash with the police. You know the world is watching us. Let's pray to God for these blessings."

The security forces had set up checkpoints on many roads and were heavily present around al-Saʿa Square and Palestinian areas. It was four forty-five in the morning. More than twenty-four hours had passed since the disappearance. During this period the police had searched the houses of many of the disappeared. Some of them and some border security personnel were astonished. Others seemed satisfied.

They didn't find a single drop of blood. They were relieved that the army either wasn't responsible for the disappearance, or it had executed it perfectly. No trace of anything except the disappearance.

Nothing in those houses indicates that their inhabitants had planned to leave them. TVs were still on in some of them, as if being watched by ghosts. Plates and tables were full of food, but the chairs were empty. When the officer in charge of the security force at the Jaffa gate saw the throngs of settlers heading toward him, he felt anxious and ordered them to stop.

Ariel was finally able to get through the masses and reach the officer to talk to him. He couldn't get his approval to accompany one of the units. Suddenly, he heard a sharp voice behind him addressing the officer. It was the settlers' leader. Ariel turned around, like a camera, and absorbed every sound and sight in the place

"Our religious duty in this sacred country obliges us to enter these houses to pray in them and reconsecrate them."

The officer tried to calm the leader at first, and explained to him that it was a closed military area and it could not be entered without authorization. But the leader's tone became more aggressive and threatening. The officer yelled and asked them to go back to where they came from, otherwise he will fire at those who disobey orders. He felt this last sentence might cost him a lot. As soon as he finished, some of the settlers' fingers were gripping the weapons they were carrying.

He hurried to calm things down. He told them they would be allowed to pray there, but without entering the houses. He radioed central command asking for more troops. Some settlers formed rings and danced. A stormy sea of humans, chanting, praying, and celebrating that this land was pure now.

Ariel left Jaffa and the voices and songs of the settlers going up to the sky behind him and went to Tel Aviv on foot.

38

Ariel

Ariel wished there'd been an elevator so he could avoid climbing the stairs. He'd walked a lot already and was tired. He got to the third floor and stood before Alaa's door. He rang the bell. He didn't know why. Then he slipped the key in the lock quickly. The light was on in the living room. His heart leapt as he craned his head in and called:

"Alaa? Alaa? Are you there?"

But then he remembered that he himself had left the light on before leaving. He walked inside the apartment nimbly and cautiously, scanning it with his gaze. He entered the bedroom and placed his bag next to the bed. He sat on the little sofa facing the bed. He turned the lamp on and remembered that he had to buy a light bulb for the one that is out in his apartment.

He noticed the jasmine next to the bed, right under the window. He didn't remember seeing it before then. Alaa was fond of Jasmine and used to talk about his grandmother's house and how it was full of Jasmine pots. He went over the day's events.

He took a deep breath and shut his eyes, as if to listen to the night's silence.

He got up and took out his laptop from his bag. He lied down on Alaa's bed and rested his back on two puffy pillows. He flipped open the laptop to check the news. He e-mailed some links to himself to read the articles in the morning. He got out of the bed and went toward Alaa's stereo. There were two shelves of CDs above it. A lot of jazz and blues, as well as Um Kulthum and Fairuz. He heard these tunes at times when he passed by Alaa's door. There was some classical music too. He chose Rimsky Korsakov.

He took off his shoes and made himself more comfortable. He tried to expel the thoughts crowding his head as he listened. Music makes the world more serene and less complicated. He regretted, for the thousandth time, that he didn't continue his piano lessons. It would've made his mother very happy.

He is too tired to go up to his apartment on the fourth floor. He almost dozed off. It feels like he hasn't slept in ages. Maybe two hours of sleep will reinvigorate him. He set the alarm next to Alaa's bed to nine in the morning. Fearing that there might be an electricity outage, he set the alarm on his cell phone as well. He took off his clothes and felt the fatigue and insomnia pulsating in his whole body. He fell asleep right away and his snoring was so loud it competed with Korsakov.

39

Ariel

The radio woke him up too early. Alaa had set it automatically to eight. Ariel was so tired he didn't understand everything the female announcer was saying. His head was spinning. He thought something must be off when he heard her say that the government has issued a decree stipulating that all residents register themselves in the nearest office. It also asked those living abroad to reregister with embassies.

He stayed in bed for a few minutes looking around with half-shut eyes. The jasmines were up too and their scent filled the room. He shook off fatigue and got up. He stood before the old wooden cabinet to the left and looked for a clean towel. All the towels were black. He smelled the biggest. It was clean.

He took off his pants and left them on the floor and went to the bathroom to take a hot shower. Some of the rings holding the shower curtain to the silver bar had detached. He liked the purple color of the shower curtain and floor mat. The soap and the washcloth were the same color. Before jumping in, he put the shower curtain rings back in place. It made him feel good. The warm shower helped shake off his sleepiness.

He reached for the black towel, dried his body, and then wrapped it around his waist. He got out of the bathroom and took his apartment key from the small nightstand next to the bed. He should've thought of getting clean clothes before taking the shower. So he headed to his apartment. He closed the door without locking it.

40

Ariel

He put on black underwear, a sky-blue shirt, and jeans. When he was about to go back to Alaa's apartment, he figured it was probably better to take a small bag and put whatever he needed in it so that he could stay there the next two days.

He packed two T-shirts, a pair of shorts, pants, and three pieces of underwear. He put in his mint-scented shampoo, toothbrush, and floss. He wasn't sure why, but he added a pack of condoms he found in the small cabinet in the bathroom. He took the food in his fridge and put it in a small grocery bag he preferred to use instead of those environmentally unfriendly plastic bags that were everywhere.

He locked the door climbed down the ten steps. He looked back at his door twice to make sure it was shut. Then he remembered the newspaper. He left the two bags next to the door and went down quickly to the ground floor. As he had hoped, the newspaper was is his mailbox. That made him smile. He stood to scan the headlines and then climbed back up to the third floor.

In the temporary apartment, as he called it, he tried to feel somewhat at home as he waited for the unknown. So, he put the feta, bread, black olives, and sausage in the fridge. Then he went to the bedroom and put the newspaper on the small round table next to the green reading sofa. He placed his other stuff on the edge of the bed and put his dirty laundry in a plastic bag. He took the tiny bag with toiletries into the bathroom and arranged its contents on the brown shelves. He went back to the green sofa, turned on the radio next to the bed, and opened the newspaper. Then he called Itzik. While on the phone, using a pen, he marked some article titles with an X to read them.

"Itzik, how are you?"

"Hi Ariel. Nothing new under the sun."

"How can there be nothing new under the sun? Don't you have some information about the disappearance and who is responsible for it? Is there anything about Titi's speech today? What of the news about these measures and the registration? I don't understand the reason behind them. Is it conceivable that these measures are taken, and you still don't know where the Palestinians have disappeared? Tell me the truth. Are the army and intelligence services somehow responsible for the matter?"

"All these questions! Calm down just a bit! The initial survey of camera footage and phone calls up till now shows a lot of strange things. But we have to analyze the data and solve the puzzle. As of now, there is no proof that we are responsible for what is taking place. At least that's what my sources confirm. It is reassuring, but we have yet to get detailed reports from the security and military intelligence. And you know that they live in their own world, as if they are states in and of themselves. The prime minister held closed meetings with the heads of apparatuses, but not much is known. We'll see."

"Come on. Do you honestly believe that? We're talking about around four million people disappearing overnight. What is going on? Do you really believe that we're not involved, or at least know about the matter?"

"Why do you think we're responsible for everything that happens to the Palestinians in this world? I'm telling you all I know in all honesty because you know how close we are and what your father meant to me."

"Ok. Fine."

"If I get any new information, I'll call you right away. Why don't you just sit at home and enjoy it. Let's be honest now. What's happening solves all our problems. You know I'm not a believer, but perhaps this is divine intervention."

Ariel laughed and said,

"We, Zionist atheists, are an off bunch. We don't believe that God exists, but we believe he performs miracles on our behalf. He doesn't exist, but we still believe he promised us this land, and now he's gotten rid of the Palestinians for us!"

Itzik laughed and then they said goodbye. Ariel was perplexed. He looked at his e-mails, reading the subject lines and only what appeared to be urgent. He clicked on Matthew's message, which was urging him to submit today's article by one in the afternoon, Tel Aviv time. He browsed Twitter and Facebook, looking for new posts and news. Then he went to the Palestinian pages he visited the day before and then to those of some Israeli and foreign friends to see if there was anything new.

The pages of Palestinians who live in the country had no posts, but they had many comments from people all over the world, asking their friends to come out and say something. Some were losing patience. The two questions that were repeated were: "Where are you? What happened to you?"

He went to the kitchen to drink water, make some coffee, and eat. There was only Turkish coffee in Alaa's kitchen. He was too lazy to go back up to his apartment to bring his coffee maker. He put three spoons of coffee in the pot and poured water and stood waiting so it wouldn't boil and spill over the stove. Alaa used to put the white cheese his mother made in jars on the shelves. Ariel got a plate to put a few pieces on. He added slices of tomatoes, cucumbers, and some of the spicy olives his mother made every year. He heated some pita too. He brought the coffee he made just the way Alaa does and went to the bedroom. He sat on the small sofa, picked up *Haaretz*, and started reading.

41

Ariel

Haaretz dedicated most of its pages to what was taking place in the country, of course. The title of the first op-ed was "Where did they go?" The second one: "Have All Our Problems Been Solves Once and For All?" The bottom half of the page had a photo of Galit, a soldier standing in a confident posture that combined femininity, strength, and liberty. She was in military fatigues with her machine gun over her shoulder. Her wavy blond hair was pulled back and her green eyes were smiling like her pink lips. The title was "The Mask Falls and Samir, the Druze, is Exposed: Interviews with Soldiers on the Battle Front. More on page 6."

The paper devoted a full page with a big photograph of the attractive soldier, who was to be the first in a series featuring interviews with soldiers who were serving in the IDF when what media outlets describes as "The Disappearance Event" took place:

HAARETZ: "Where were you when you learned of the disappearance of the Palestinians?"

GALIT: "I was on a night shift at Qalan-
dya checkpoint. Samir, a Druze from Daliyat
al-Karmil, was with us that night. He was in
charge of searching the cars coming through. I
don't remember what time it was, but he said he
was going to the toilet and would return soon. I
took his position. There wasn't a lot of traffic late
at night. So I didn't pay attention to his absence at
first. But when he was gone for half an hour, I was
worried. I went looking for him and was shocked
when I saw his weapon thrown next to the toilet.
I informed the CO right away and tried to secure
the area. I thought he had been kidnapped.

"Additional troops were sent. Then we
realized that others had disappeared too. Imagine, I was worried about him as a colleague, and
was thinking of various possible scenarios about
Arabs kidnapping and torturing him. And after
all that worrying I discovered that he had just
run away and left his weapon so irresponsibly. I
don't understand why the Druze would run away
with the Arabs?"

HAARETZ: "Were there no signs at all that
Samir was about to run away and disappear?"

GALIT: "I didn't sense anything. He liked
and enjoyed serving in the army. Frankly, Arabs
are violent and although he was Druze, he was
like them. I don't know where all this violence
comes from? Frankly, and in my experience, I
find that many of the minorities who serve with
us enjoy searching Palestinians. And now they
betray us and run away. How can we trust them

after today? We break our backs and try to make things easier for Palestinians crossing the border, who are stubborn and cause all kinds of problems and chaos. Some even smell awful and their cars are dirty. Samir knew how to deal with them, and when he yelled at them in Arabic, they would be quiet. They stand there quietly. I think that's the only language they understand. Yelling. We try to say 'please,' and we often forget, but not intentionally. Anyway, we try to treat them humanely, but they make things difficult. We tell them a thousand times a day that they have to wait in line, but they crowd. When I watch them standing at the checkpoint I feel the desire for killing and revenge in their eyes. You can see the hostility in their eyes."

HAARETZ: "How do you feel now? Having trusted someone like Samir and trained with him and then you discover he is someone else?"

GALIT: "I couldn't sleep at first, especially when it became clear that the Arabs had disap- peared, and we didn't know who was responsible for kidnapping them or what exactly had hap- pened. First I blamed us. You know we are highly self-critical and even masochists. Sometimes we blame ourselves for things we are not guilty of. But that's normal, because we are victims and have been hunted for hundreds, even thousands of years. But we were able to protect ourselves despite everything that we went through. The question that puzzles me is: Why do Palestinian mothers send their children to throw stones and

carry out terrorist attacks against us? I never
understood why they insisted on coming to the
checkpoints every day to fight us? Maybe they
have some sadism because their society is prim-
itive and violent. I don't know, but from my
experience as a soldier, I feel they like to either be
beaten and tortured, or to hit and insult others. Otherwise, I have no explanation for their
insistence on all this violence. Maybe it's in their
history and identity, or from their families and
the environment they grow up in. Whatever it is,
I just hope they leave us alone so we can continue
to build our country, and so that peace reigns in
the world, and in the new middle east. We will
be able to help a lot of Arab countries with our
knowledge and the technology we have. Israeli
'know-how' and Arab capital. If we unite with
the Arabs, a lot of good will come out, and we
can teach them a great deal."

❧

Ariel read the interview carefully and underlined
some of the sentences he might use in his next article. Dan Rubenstein's article surprised him. The vet-
eran communist had been relatively sidelined because
many find him to be an extremist leftist.

AND THE WINNER IS: ISRAEL!
Dan Rubenstein

Were there prizes given out to the most modern
and most racist state, that calls itself "democratic,"

this country would have won first place. Is this the Zionist dream you wanted? I write "you," because, as everyone knows, I have divorced Zionism and no longer believe in it.

We have over indulged ourselves in pain as victims, and have forgotten that we are human and that Europe is not the middle east. What happened to the reasonable ones in you, my country? Were they killed, or they, too, have left you with the Palestinians? Can we ever rid ourselves of the victim complex? We are no longer victims. We must say that out loud. We have become normal humans in a state.

Where to start from? Since we established this state we have been digging our graves with our own hands. Are we implementing the settlers' agenda and fulfilling their dreams? They are the state's first enemies. How can a state with this number of surveillance camera everywhere not know where more than four million Palestinians have gone?

We are responsible for anything that happens to them. They, both citizens and those living the occupied territories, were under the protection of the state. The United Nations charter and International Law stipulate the responsibility of occupying powers to protect unarmed civilians.

I have warned time and again against racist and discriminatory policies and the danger of not recognizing the historic mistakes that were committed by organizations when the state was founded, and by the successive governments.

But no one listened to me personally, or listened to other voices. On the contrary, an unrelenting war was waged against us. And it wasn't limited to name-calling. I was personally threatened, attacked, and beaten after giving lectures. All this took place before the eyes of the police who are supposed to provide protection.

Just a few hours after the first official announcement about the disappearance of the Arabs, I received a call from the police. They wanted to interrogate me. Why? Because I am a "friend" of the Palestinians. The security forces don't know where they have gone? Is that conceivable? Who will believe that? Is this the first step in putting the Left, which is almost extinct in this country, on trial? Are we now responsible for what might be the "cleanest" campaign of ethnic cleansing witnessed by humanity?

I can no longer bear what is happening in this country. It is no longer possible to live in a country where the desire to eliminate the other has reached the level of genocide. It is no longer possible to believe in tolerance, or dialogue, because there is no one left to have a dialogue with.

We are still not sure yet. However, if it is proven that the government is responsible for this operation, this means we have carried out a suicide mission to finish ourselves, first and foremost. It is no longer important henceforth who is responsible for the disappearance of the Palestinians. Whether they left "out of their own volition" as some officials try to hint, or whether we have been able to

eliminate them in a way no else has been able to do
before, what we must do now is . . .

🖎

Ariel stopped reading and put the newspaper away
once he heard on the radio that Prime Minister Titi's
speech has started. He turned on the TV and turned
down the radio.

42

Ariel

The prime minister was delivering his speech before a group of Knesset members and some officers who had attended this extraordinary session. He and they appeared self-composed.

"Ladies and Gentlemen, sons and daughters of this generous people, I address you from the podium of freedom in the only true democracy in the entire region. Despite what neighboring countries have witnessed, their elections and parliaments cannot compare to, or compete with, the history of this deep-rooted parliament and its young democracy. Our country is going through a difficult period that is even more dangerous than that during which we declared our independence in 1948. This exceptional situation calls for exceptional measures and for unity among all forces, from the left to the right. There is no right and left after today. No secular and religious. We are all one hand.

"Our country is being subjected to a campaign that no other country has witnessed in the past. It is the first of its kind. If the disappearance of the

Palestinians indicates anything, then it is that a heinous conspiracy is being hatched against us. When the founding fathers established our state, they enacted laws and carried out measures. Time has proven their foresight and significance. Today we have issued orders and are about to enact laws that will protect us. In this state of extreme emergency, we have declared that we have to move in an unusually swift manner to deal with this exceptional circumstance we are going through.

"All citizens must register with the state's census offices. I, personally, was one of the first to do so. These steps are necessary to ascertain the identity of all those present in the country. Those residing abroad, or currently travelling, should register at our embassies wherever they happen to be as soon as possible. In the next few hours we will count and register everyone. Anyone whose name doesn't appear, or who doesn't return within forty-eight hours of the first cases of disappearance by Arabs, meaning by 3 a.m. tomorrow, will not be allowed to return. Their property shall be transferred to the state.

"We will not tolerate or accept any returnees. Whoever is not in the country by 3 a.m. will lose his or her right to be in this place and any access to it.

"They have disappeared out of their own volition. We did not expel anyone and no one can prove otherwise. I held a long meeting today with the minister of security and leaders of the army, police, and intelligence. Footage from surveillance cameras in public places has not revealed any unusual movement. It is truly perplexing and that is why we declared a state of maximum emergency in order to protect the country from any conspiracy. After consulting with our allies, we have taken several measures. Some of which we have declared and others will be in due course.

"We would like to know where they have gone, but, at the end of the day, it is their decision. We have not forced anyone to leave. Irrespective of the reason for which they chose to leave, they did so as others have and went back to their countries.

"Today we must be vigilant and stop pointing fingers at each other. Some on the left think that our government is responsible for the disappearance of the Palestinians. Such naïveté can be destructive and it only helps our enemies. We must be careful. We are in communication with our neighbors to reach an agreement on settling the Arabs who left Israel in 1948 and who call themselves Palestinians. This is up to them, but we must protect our borders. We will not allow an ant to cross them without our permission.

"Fellow citizens, may God help us in this crisis. Let us stand together as one and may there be peace in Israel and the world at large. . . . Amen."

*

Ariel had misgivings as he listened to the speech. It was as if the entire country stood before a traffic light waiting for the green sign to go. To go toward the unknown, which seems better. The phone rang. It was his mother.

"*Boker Tov*, Ariel."

"*Boker Tov.* I was thinking of calling you. How was your night?"

"I feel somewhat better after hearing Titi's speech. Let's see what is going to happen. Why didn't you come to see me yesterday as you promised?"

"I'm sorry. I should've called. But I was crushed by work and needed time to think and read. I'll pass by tonight for sure."

"No need to. I'm going to Haifa. They say one can go to Wadi al-Nisnas and see the Arab houses there, and even buy one very cheap."

"Who said that?"

"Judith called from Haifa and she knows an influential guy in the army. He said they'll announce it. Do you remember the houses on Abbas Street? They are lovely and they overlook the sea. Maybe we can get one there."

"I don't think it's true. We still don't know what's going on. I think it's best if you stay here in Tel Aviv, near me. I'll come and sleep over tonight or tomorrow. Or you can come to my apartment and sleep there. I'm sleeping in Alaa's now."

"I don't want to stay in Tel Aviv. I want to go somewhere that's more quiet. And if the news is true, I want us to choose a house there. I had been eyeing a house on Abbas Street. You know that I love

the weather in Haifa much more than Tel Aviv. It's
beautiful and quiet. Why are you sleeping in Alaa's
apartment anyway?"

"You are stubborn, mother, and it's difficult to
argue once you've made up your mind. Have a good
time then and give me a call once you get there."

"*Nishmaa.*"

"*Nishmaa.*"

He heard noise coming from outside so he headed
to the window. He couldn't see much from his balcony. He went back to the room and got his keys,
phone, and wallet, and went out to the street.

43

Rothschild Boulevard

Preparations were underway for the biggest festival in the young country's history in the White City. Yesterday is far behind, and today will pass quickly. In modern states people chase the future. The victors never look back. They only look forward. Forward march! Like tank tracks, their steps march to their target even if the path is circular, or zigzag. They march to their target and prepare the path for the future.

Municipal workers in the city and elsewhere in the country were removing the signs that had street and city names written in Arabic. Everything will be in Hebrew tonight. Together with English, which is acceptable.

In the middle of the expansive and verdant Rothschild Boulevard, workers were extending electric cords, punctuated by colorful lights, and adorned with blue and white flags. Other groups were erecting platforms on Rothschild and in other streets and squares in the city. Decorations were being hung on trees. Children ran around joyously because the following day was going to be a public holiday.

Music billowed from the cars roaming the city as if expelling the remaining silence from its streets.

44

Ariel

Tel Aviv—Ariel Levy

After being halted for more than forty hours, it was just announced that air traffic will resume gradually as of four o'clock tomorrow morning. This indicates that, while still in a state of maximum emergency, security officials now feel that the danger is limited, and can be brought under control. Tomorrow will be a public holiday for schools and state institutions, but shops are expected to be open.

I can hear the music outside my apartment. I returned just a while ago after walking around Tel Aviv to see what is going on firsthand. Municipality workers are hanging decorations. But some are warning about the assaults taking place against those thought to be Arabs. It seems they turned out to be Mizrahi. The chief of police tried to calm everyone to make sure panic and mutual suspicion don't spread. What has bothered some is the settlers leaving the vast land in the territories and coming with the intent to take control of cities and villages inside what used to be the Green Line.

The government has yet to offer any suggestions or solutions as to what is to become of the houses in these areas. In a few hours it will have been forty hours since the disappearance. If they don't return in these remaining hours, they will no longer have the right to return to the country according to the law of the "disappeared" which was ratified rather swiftly today.

In just a few hours the country has moved from one era to another. Some speculate that what has taken place is merely the magician's tricks backfiring against him, as the proverb says. Initial signs indicate that the Palestinians themselves, or some of their leaders, planned this thing. Everyone succumbed and it seems many were forced to. The coming days and months will reveal what we still don't know for sure.

At 1 p.m., Fuad Namir, the minister of defense, ended a press conference attended by representatives of several ministries as well as security chiefs. He assured citizens and our neighbors that the government is in control of the situation. He stressed the government's desire to strengthen relations with its neighbors, especially since there are no longer any obstacles. While it is still not clear what will happen to Palestinians in these neighboring states, "We view that as an internal matter. We will not interfere, but will help in resettling them if needed." He added that neighboring countries are aware of our military capacity, as well as that of our allies who stand with us. Some neighboring countries have declared a state of emergency in anticipation of any trouble. The United States and EU countries have bolstered security measures in their airports.

Responding to a question about the situation at the borders, the defense minister confirmed that there was no unusual military movement except for a few attempts to infiltrate from neighboring countries by individuals thought to be of Palestinian origins. "We are searching for them, but have not found any traces inside the country. It seems that they disappear as soon as they infiltrate the border."

I spoke to some Israelis in Tel Aviv. Danny, who owns a kiosk that sells newspapers and coffee on Dezingoff Street, said, "I am very disappointed by this treason. It looks like the Palestinians decided to disappear, or were planning something and couldn't do it. I had a lot of Arab friends. I used to eat hummus and falafel in Jaffa, and even smoke shisha sometimes. I don't understand why they did this to us? They plan an operation that fails and then leave us by ourselves. I used to think that we could at least trust Israeli Arabs, but things are clear now."

Daphna, a thirty-five-year-old teacher from Ramat Aviv, said, "It's difficult to believe that the Palestinians have disappeared without us having a hand in the matter. The problem now is what can we, as residents, do? We don't have enough information to pressure the government." Daron, a guard at a huge mall on Dezingoff, said he is overjoyed because the problem that is called "Palestinians" has resolved itself. He added, "At last we have gotten rid of those black snakes." The majority are silent and awaiting instructions. But I sensed relief among many that there is no proof so far that the IDF is involved in the disappearance.

In a few hours, this exceptional country will enter a new phase in its miraculous history. A history that started with a miracle and is now being fortified by another.

Ariel reviewed the article more than once as usual and changed a few sentences. He felt odd that he was so relieved, but didn't dwell on it.

45

Ariel

There was a lot of chatter on the radio. He called his mother to check on her and see how things were in Haifa. "Ima, Ariel . . . Tov. I'm not sure if you're already in Haifa, or on your way there? Call me as soon as you get this. Miss you."

He went back to the notebook he'd left on the table next to the sofa early that morning. He picked it up and sat in bed, resting his back on the puffy pillows. He craved some red wine. He put the notebook aside and got up and went to the kitchen. He looked in Alaa's cabinets and found a Californian cabernet. There was a wine opener was in one of the small drawers. He opened another cabinet and took out one of the big glasses Alaa was fond of buying. He went back to the bedroom and put both bottle and glass on the nightstand. He took off his shoes, got his laptop, and lay down. He took the red notebook into his lap. The radio kept him company. He created a new file on his laptop, named it "Chronicle of Pre-Disappearance," and began selecting excerpts from Alaa's notebook to translate

to Hebrew. He thought they could be part of a book
he will write and publish on the disappearance of
the Palestinians.

46

Alaa

I couldn't sleep. It's six in the morning. I think of you a lot. Actually, in the beginning, when I lay down on the sofa in the living room, listening to the radio and looking out of the window, I didn't think of you a lot. But then I saw the old sewing machine you used to work on and live off until a few years before your death. Mother used to be angry with you. She would say that our situation was good and my father's work secured a life better than most of those around us. But you refused to give up sewing and be dependent on your son-in-law. I asked you once why you never stopped sewing. Was there something more than just not wanting to depend on my father? You said you felt you were like family to all those brides. That women used to come to you for help because their families were forced to leave and they stayed, together with their husbands, with those who stole the country. You often said "they" without mentioning who they were. You told me about Abla, our neighbor, who came knocking on your door when she was still fifteen. She ran barefoot, crying and saying that her father had come back home drunk. She begged you to go with her so that he wouldn't fight with her mother. Her mother had no family or relatives of her own in Jaffa. She didn't know to whom she could turn. You were her family. You went with her and spent the night at their house so her parents wouldn't fight. It is for the sake of these people and for your own that you kept on sewing. Survivors are the loneliest. Despite all the stories, it's difficult at times for me to imagine what you felt those first days after the nakba. When the extent of the damage left by the flood became clear. That is how I imagine the scene. A scene that has yet to end.

Survivors are the loneliest. Yesterday I read that one of Jaffa's names is "The Stranger's Mother." Maybe that is the reason the city spat us out. Because we are no longer strangers in it. Perhaps we will return to it now because we have become strangers to it while in it or outside. Do inanimate objects have a memory? Do the things around us have a memory? Does the sewing machine have a memory? Does it remember your feet, tears, fears, and the long hours you spent behind it? Does it remember the stories of the brides and the women who came to you to sew their dresses and who told you their stories?

I miss you a lot and I miss my father. Father committed suicide. Yes, suicide. We didn't tell anyone, because it was shameful and *haram*. But I have stopped lying. When someone asked me about him recently, I said that he committed suicide. At first

I said he "passed away" and he offered his condolences. I was silent for twenty seconds that felt like ten minutes, then I said it. He said it's unbecoming of me to say that about him. I laughed and told him it's the truth. Do you know what he said to me? "God help everybody."

I miss you. Missing you is like a rose of thorns.

47

Ariel

The sun had set and night awakened. Ariel woke up when the music outside got louder. He looked at his cell phone. It was ten thirty. He got out of bed and went to the bathroom to wash his face. He came back to bed and gulped the rest of the wine. He pressed the button to listen to Uncle Itzik's voicemail.

"Shalom Ariel. Itzik here. Call me when you get this, or early in the morning. I have some important news. A scoop for you."

Ariel called him, but his phone was turned off. He didn't leave a message. He'll call him again. Jonathan said that they were expecting an analytical piece from him at the newspaper by six in the morning, New York time. His mother called to let him know she's fine. There were other calls from friends in the country and from abroad. Everyone wants to make sure he's safe.

He went out to the balcony. The platforms and decorations were in place and flags everywhere. What if the Palestinians return before 3 a.m., he thought? What if they return before the deadline we set for them? What if they didn't adhere to our times and chose the time themselves?

He took a deep breath and sighed. He went back inside, headed to the kitchen, and poured water in a big glass. He took in the place around him. The apartment needs a coat of paint. He went back to bed and turned on some jazz on his laptop and kept the news on in the background. He looked at the screen and went over the notes he'd jotted down, and some of the sentences he had translated. He poured some more wine and sipped it. He logged into his Twitter account to read what news agencies and international newspapers, including Arab and Israeli, were tweeting. He scrolled through tens of tweets. Nothing new. Most of them start out with "breaking" but soon thereafter are refuted or turn out to be sensationalist chatter to attract readers. He looked at his watch anxiously. He created a new file on his laptop and started a to-do list for the coming few days. Then he went back to read Alaa's notebook and take notes.

48

Alaa

I sit down and miss you. But today, for the first time, I smiled when I was missing you. Only because I remembered why I loved you more than anyone else. Do you know why? Because you loved life and never lost hope. You learned to love Jaffa even when it was cruel and you taught me that love. You used to say that Jaffans are sea people and merchants. They acclimate no matter where they go or stay, like shore people. You were alone in Jaffa, but you loved it like you loved a man madly. You wouldn't stop loving no matter what. I sit in the small courtyard in your house. I have repaired it and painted it. I didn't get a permit from the municipality. We'll see how they react. I watered your jasmines. Their scent is all around. Like you, jasmines love the night. The moon is so full and big tonight. It's about to take up the whole sky. I don't know why I feel so happy today. As if I've rediscovered Jaffa, or learned to love it again. I walk and see its beauty. I don't forget you, but I see its beauty. I don't forget its memory, but, nevertheless, I see its beauty. I remembered that sentence you repeated so often: "Oh my, Jaffa is so beautiful and Palestine is so beautiful! Very beautiful and it's not lost.

"That year is gone. But we are still here, grandson. Look how beautiful these jasmines are! Rights are never lost as long as one demands them." I hope you are right. Who knows? But, yes, Jaffa is so beautiful.

I brought a bottle of local arak. It's lethal. Don't be upset that am drinking arak in your house. I'm listening to that Um Kulthum song you loved so much. Do you remember? "Far from you . . ." I long for you as I listen to it, and longing is love. Here's to you and to Palestine. Oh, how beautiful is Palestine.

49

Ariel

He was translating some of what Alaa had written when he heard a rattle outside. He didn't pay any attention to it at first. It's probably a homeless man scavenging the trash, or a cat. But it was a stubborn rattle. He stopped writing, turned down the music and the radio, and went out to the balcony. He looked at the adjacent buildings, the street, and looked down at the trash bins. Everything was quiet, as if in a state of anticipation. Only two hours left till 3 a.m. He went back in to the living room through the other door in the balcony. He touched the wall looking for the light switch to turn it on. He scanned the room, walked through the apartment, and looked behind the doors. Perhaps a mouse had gotten inside? But there was no trace of anything anywhere. The rattle subsided and then disappeared. As if it were a whisper. He went back to bed. As soon as he started reading Alaa's notebook, he heard a whisper. He went out to the balcony again looking for the source. Then he went to the door and looked through the keyhole before opening it and craning his head. He turned on the stair light. He looked in all directions. Nothing.

He locked the door it and went back to bed. He remembered his English grandmother who always complained about hearing whispers at night. He looked at his phone. It was 2 a.m. He stretched out on the bed and looked at the to-do list. He has to change the apartment's door lock. He wrote that down and underlined it. The next day was a public holiday, but shops will probably be open. Even if the locksmith isn't open, he'll call the owner and ask him to come and change the lock. Changing the door lock. He has to change the door lock. That sentence was pecking his dream. He fell asleep before the clock struck three in the morning.

The red notebook is still open.

⇒ T H E   E N D ⇐

Afterword

> The loneliness of the Palestinian [in
> Israel] . . . is the greatest loneliness of all.
> —Anton Shammas, *Arabesque*

The Book of Disappearance is a novel about the Palestinians who survived the nakba of 1948 and remained in Palestine. They did not become refugees, like those who are still scattered in a vast diaspora and in refugee camps in Palestine itself and in neighboring countries. Those who survived inside Palestine live(d) (under military rule until 1966) as second-class citizens in the state of Israel. The author herself is a descendant of those survivors. One branch of her family was forced out of their home in Jaffa and were internally displaced. Her short stories and novels (*Sifr al-Ikhtifa'*; *The Book of Disappearance* is her second) are informed by imagination, of course, but by living memories and visceral personal experiences too.

"Survivors are lonely," writes Alaa, one of the two main narrators in the novel, when he remembers his late grandmother. He, too, suffers from and has inherited a version of this immense loneliness. Because he lives in the ruins and remains of a Palestine that *was*. A Palestine that survived intact only in his grandmother's memory. He, after all, was born in the state of Israel, a settler-colonial state premised on the destruction of Palestine and the negation of the existence and history of its indigenous population. More than 400 villages were destroyed and/or depopulated in 1948 and 750,000 Palestinians were expelled from their homes.[1] Major Palestinian cities that were the centers of a dynamic and integrated sociocultural life were occupied and their populations forced to flee. A small percentage of those who remained were herded into fenced neighborhoods (this is what happens to the grandmother and her generation). The Israeli state erased neighborhood and street names and replaced them with new ones. Israel cannibalized Palestinian land and property.

The stories Alaa's grandmother recounts and the characters in them inhabit a Jaffa and a Palestine Alaa struggles to recognize. The sense of acute alienation a Palestinian inside Israel feels, particularly one who knew and lived in Palestine before 1948, is poignantly crystallized in the grandmother's statement: "I walk in the city, but it doesn't recognize me." The

---

1. For more, see Illan Pappe, *The Ethnic Cleansing of Palestine* (OneWorld Publications, 2006).

relationship with one's surroundings is disfigured and forever severed.

There are two Jaffas, Alaa writes. "Your Jaffa resembles mine, but it is not the same. Two cities impersonating each another. You carved your names in my city and so I feel like I am a returnee from history. Always tired, roaming my own life like a ghost. Yes, I am a ghost who lives in your city. You, too, are a ghost, living in my city. We call both cities 'Jaffa.'"

Only belatedly, and retroactively, does Alaa begin to fully understand his grandmother's trauma and that of her generation. He begins to actively *un*learn and debunk the official Zionist history he had to internalize in the educational system to pass. He preserves his grandmother's memory and deploys it as an oral history to counter and resist Zionist history and the official narrative of the colonial state—a narrative where he is, for all intents and purposes, absent. The Palestinians who were displaced from their villages in 1948 and who were internally displaced were designated by Israeli law as "present-absentees." Alaa removes street signs and crosses out colonial nomenclature, giving streets (back) their Palestinian names.

The central event that triggers and sustains the narrative structure of the novel is the inexplicable disappearance of all Palestinians. The effects of this event on Israelis and the spectrum of reactions and responses in the forty-eight hours that follow occupies a significant part of the novel. What the author imagines and narrates is the colonial fantasy par excellence. The most often quoted motto in Zionist discourse is, "A land without a people for a people without a land." Zionist leaders in the last century have offered variations on this theme. Golda Meir (1898–1978), who was the prime minister of Israel from 1969 to 1974, stated that "[t]here is no such thing as Palestinians." Another prime minister, Yitzhak Rabin (1922–1995) hoped that "Gaza would sink into the sea." The native as a nuisance, obstacle, and threat is a typical colonial trope. But the natives' total disappearance is as disquieting and threatening as their presence. One is reminded of Cavafy's lines in "Waiting for the Barbarians": "Now what's going to happen to us without barbarians/Those people were a kind of solution."

The Israeli responses to the disappearance range from indignation and feelings of betrayal to relief and joy. If the religious zealots rejoice and consider the disappearance a miracle, the secular liberals, believers in the state's secular miracles, think it is a military or intelligence operation. There is also the lone voice of the radical leftist, an endangered species.

Ariel's mother doesn't sing and dance to celebrate divine intervention, but she goes to Haifa to find one of those empty beautiful houses "abandoned" by the absent Palestinians. Ariel is uncomfortable with the vulgarity of the settlers who rush to occupy and consecrate the spaces vacated by Palestinians. But it doesn't take him too long to feel at home in Alaa's apartment. He sleeps there to wait and see, but as the state's deadline approaches, he seems to be comfortable in his friend's place and we can assume that he will make it his own.

The material and discursive colonization of the geographic place called Palestine continues. The nakba, "that year" as Alaa's grandmother calls it, is still ongoing in its effects and practices. Having taken over the land and the houses and changed the names, what remains to be usurped is memory, collective and individual. But memory is the last trench and refuge, and a space that cannot be expropriated by law or force.

"The old will die and the young will forget," is a saying attributed to David Ben Gurion (1886–1973) about how Palestinians will react to Israel. The grandmother's death and Alaa's longing for her compel him to start writing. He writes in his journal to recall his conversations with her, maintain the bond, and remember Jaffa and Palestine. The old have died, but the young have not forgotten and will not forget—this is what Alaa demonstrates. His red notebook, like the novel's end, remains open.

The ghosts of the dead will continue to haunt, demanding justice and recognition, and the living will write and remember.

Ariel wants to appropriate Alaa's words and memories and claim the narrative as his own. This novel itself is another red notebook, but it has not fallen (exclusively) into Ariel's hands. It will be open for all to read. Art here achieves one of its most powerful effects: preserving memory and defending life with beauty.

Sinan Antoon
October 2018, New York

Ibtisam Azem is a Palestinian novelist and journalist. She has published two novels in Arabic: *Sariq al-Nawm* (*The Sleep Thief*, 2011) and *Sifr al-Ikhtifaa* (*The Book of Disappearance*, 2014), both by Dar al-Jamal (Beirut/Baghdad). She was born and raised in Taybeh, northern Jaffa, and studied at the Hebrew University of Jerusalem and later at Freiburg University in Germany, where she completed an MA in German and English Literature and Islamic Studies. She is senior correspondent in New York for the Arabic daily *al-Araby al-Jadeed*. She is currently working on an MA at the Silver School of Social Work at New York University.

Sinan Antoon is a poet, novelist, and translator. He holds degrees from Baghdad, Georgetown, and Harvard, where he specialized in Arabic literature. His books include *I'jaam*, *The Corpse Washer*, *The Baghdad Eucharist*, and *The Book of Collateral Damage*. His translation of Mahmoud Darwish's *In the Presence of Absence* won the 2012 American Literary Translators' Award. He is an associate professor at New York University.

Printed in the USA
CPSIA information can be obtained
at www.ICGtesting.com
CBHW070230110324
5155CB00003B/3

9 780815 611110